BEST
LESBIAN EROTICA
OF THE YEAR

VOLUME FIVE

BEST
LESBIAN EROTICA
OF THE YEAR

VOLUME FIVE

Edited by
SINCLAIR SEXSMITH

CLEIS
PRESS

Published in the United States by Cleis Press, an imprint of Start Midnight, LLC, 221 River Street, 9th Floor, Hoboken, NJ 07030.

Printed in the United States.
Cover design: Allyson Fields
Cover photograph: Shutterstock
Text design: Frank Wiedemann

First Edition.
10 9 8 7 6 5 4 3 2 1

Trade paper ISBN: 978-1-62778-308-8
E-book ISBN: 978-1-62778-521-1

for my boy

CONTENTS

I love reading erotica. It thrills me in the way only words strung together in cadence and rhythm and assonance can; it drops me to my knees, with relief in the expression that I understand, I feel, I know, I connect.

It is the relief that I'm not alone.

And, not to get personal here but, I love sex. I love the magic of our sensate bodies, how they fit together, what it's like to touch and be touched, to smell and see and hear and taste, to be as close to another as we really possibly can be, to even be inside one another.

But erotica isn't only about sex. In fact, some of the most erotic writing I've ever read doesn't describe a single sex act—it might just describe something extra-sensorial, something sensuous, something full of longing or want or anticipation.

"Erotic" can be far more than just sex, far more than genitals touching, mouths touching, hands touching. It still usually has to do with our bodies, with our senses—luscious food can be erotic, incredible art can be erotic, smacking the ball with the center of the bat to make that perfect arc way into the outfield can be erotic.

All kinds of things elicit something akin to an erotic response.

This collection of stories is a meditation expanding on the idea of what eroticism is. Is it imagining touching, energetically connecting? Is it pleasing another? Is it service? Is it blood? Is it tender kissing? Is it an emotionally secure enough attachment to one up the relationship? Is it not knowing whose body parts are whose? Is it pain, is it fear?

The characters in this book explore all kinds of erotic encounters, finding refuge, finding connection, and finding themselves.

Wherever you are in your exploration of sexuality, of eros, and of queer sex, I hope you find something deliciously erotic in here.

Sinclair Sexsmith
February 2020

MAX AND THE THINGS
I COULDN'T SAY

Heart

"Is this your first time at a party like this?" I asked, but I already knew the answer. She nodded slowly and I watched her eyes follow another beautiful femme babe in lingerie. It's a dream really, a sapphic slumber party full of playful kinky queer women in various stages of undress. Everyone is flirting. There's a guest in a leather corset with a curvy belle over her knee, spanks and squeals fill the room as the buzz of a Hitachi Magic Wand adds to the general thrill of the evening. Prosecco is being poured, wooden paddles are being pulled out of bags and eyed excitedly, the two ladies who showed up unexpectedly wearing matching silk robes were now curled up on a loveseat making out. I smirked watching Max take it all in. Her arms, tattooed and muscular, caught my attention when she arrived, looking a little out of place. She had an undeniable charm, somehow she had me feeling her thigh muscles and getting flustered within moments of meeting her. I could tell she worked with her hands, I couldn't stop staring at them.

* * *

I wanted to say: "How are you so fucking hot? Wanna put your hands on me?"

Instead I said: "I'll be back, I gotta go lend a hand in the kitchen."

She hooked up with someone else that night, but she made an impression. Almost every beauty there asked about her once she'd disappeared. Typical, right? Thirty-four feminine dolls in a room and we all throw ourselves at the one beautiful butch who was brave enough to attend.

I was glad when our paths crossed again. I was glad I found the courage to confess I had a crush on her. I stumbled and stammered trying to explain that I was terrible at making the first move. I was glad when she put me out of my misery and pulled me towards her for a kiss.

She unzipped my sundress so delicately. She fawned over me as she undressed me, piece by piece. I hadn't been intimate with someone new in a long time. She made it easy. "You look so fucking good naked," she said as she squeezed my thighs. She was all soft kisses and hard abs, tattoos trailing across her hips.

I still get shivers when I think of how she pulled me on top of her before I could get her pants off and made me grind against her. Her hands firm on my hips, guiding me, my hair wild and sticking to our sweat and our wet mouths, her breath catching in her throat, my little whimpers. I blushed when I saw the slippery wet spot I left on her zipper fly.

She likes simple things: my long dark hair tumbling over my shoulders, sweetly asking me to sit on her face, spoiling me rotten.

We fucked for hours. It was so fucking good. And then we got dressed, went downstairs for a smoke, and went back up to her hotel room so she could undress me all over again.

* * *

"Tell me the mean things you like," she said as she gently kissed my collarbone after making me come for the third time. We spend all of our dates in bed. She's not mean. She's tender and careful. Kink is foreign to her, but she's so eager to please me.

I hid my face, ashamed of my masochism. "I don't want to say them."

She said she wouldn't judge. She said, "What's your favorite mean thing?" She said, "Just tell me one."

I didn't want to tell her, I didn't want her to think she had to do anything differently. I felt exposed, afraid to spill secrets. She just wanted to make me feel good. She just wanted to worship me in all the ways I enjoy.

"What do you like?" she asked, her eyes are my favorite color of green, that silvery sage color, it matches the streak in my hair. It's hard not to love her right away.

I wanted to say: "I like being destroyed. I like being ripped apart at the seams. Shake me, rattle my bones, force me open. I want to feel you for days, I want your teeth and fists to make an impression. Make me forget the best of you. Make me forget my own name, my history, my mother tongue. I can take it, this current of pain, I can absorb it all and turn it into something fucking beautiful. Give me everything you can, watch my jaw clench and tremble, watch my back arch, watch my eyes squeeze shut. I'm your doll, your punching bag, your prize. When I cry for you, you'll know I mean it."

But that's not her language. She doesn't want those things, they don't translate for her. Her language is worshipping every inch of my soft curves, opening the car door for me, and making sure there's lemonade in her fridge. Her language is calm and loyal and reassuring. Her language is beautiful. Her language is the way she looks at me like she sees something marvelous, how the corners of her mouth twitch and dance if I stare at her too long, like I'm making her nervous but she can't look away. This kind of adoration is foreign, a warm amber light washing over me.

So instead I said: "I like *you*," parting my thighs so she could get closer.

It felt too daunting to start listing the complicated ways pain and suffering entwine with pleasure, too vulnerable when these strange desires weren't shared. My kinks are a list of things that are hard to own and understand. I like being overwhelmed. I like to be scared. I like punching and forcing and fisting, all things that feel extreme. I like words she's never heard before like waterboard, bastinado, and cuckquean. I like trying to come while I'm struggling to breathe. I like playing with jealousy and real hurts and insecurities. I like edges. Those things are hard to explain. They're not tidy packages. They're not easy to swallow. I didn't want to say them out loud, or burden her with knowing they exist. But she's given me acceptance and adoration, no reason to shy away.

"I like you too," she said, and I believed her.

We are opposites in so many ways: I worry and she is unruffled, she works with her hands and I work in words, I never shut up and she does most of her talking with her eyes. She's so quiet, I make more noise than she does when I'm giving her head. I listen to her breathing for cues, follow the subtle twitching of her thighs as I gently suck on her swollen clit and moan a little against her wetness. She's dripping and she tastes so good. I love being on my knees for her, I love showing her my devotion. I know I'm doing a good job when she gently places her hand on my head and presses against me. Steady. So steady. Her tender touches melt me, even in this moment when my tongue is buried in her cunt. She brushes my hair softly out of my eyes and tucks it behind my ear so she can see my face. I can feel my cheeks turning pink, the way she looks down at me as I kneel between her legs makes my heart thump faster.

I want to text her the next morning to say:

"All the words to worship you haven't been invented yet. My tongue hasn't found them. I stumble across all the words I know, and the closest one I have is 'Good.' And baby, I'm wearing that one out. I say it a thousand times, you're so good, too good, taste good, feel good, real good, your face is so good, you're so, so good. Good with a capital G. Good to the bone. It's the closest truth. I'm learning new words though, just so I can whisper them to you when I'm breathless and you're keeping me warm. You're so good to me, so good my heart's in my throat, and my mouth can't do this feeling justice."

Instead I say: "You're on my mind."

I wanted to take her picture. Seeing her disarmed, her face relaxed, her eyes warm, made me want to freeze this moment in time. Her face is so good, I try to memorize it. Her light brown hair is short and scattered with silver. I love to run my fingertips along the sides. Her fresh cut shows off her strong brow and dark lashes, faint freckles dust her cheeks and the bridge of her nose. There's a small beauty mark on her cheekbone, and she has perfect teeth. Her silver-green eyes squinch up when she laughs. I wanted to wake up tomorrow and be able to study her face again, even if she was at work and I was busy in my own world. She has this harmonious balance of dark and light. She's beautiful and handsome.

She hates photos. She doesn't take selfies. When she was traveling I asked her to send me one and she sent a pic of her forearm, all flexed and veiny, "All's fair in love and war" tattooed in cursive. (Well played.)

She doesn't like the camera in her face. She twitches when I tell her how badly I'd like to capture how she looks. I play with this edge.

"How much would you protest if I grabbed my phone and took a picture of us?" It's still too early for me to read how much of an invasion this is for her. I tread lightly as she hesitates to give me the answer I'm looking for. I kiss her and giggle. "Poor Max," I chide, as I kiss her cheek, and trail my kisses down her neck. "What if I promise to spoil you afterwards?" She smiles when I say this, and I know I've won. I cover her face in kisses, "Now that I know your currency I'm unstoppable," I proclaim.

I grab my phone and snuggle up in the crook of her arm, flipping to the front camera and quickly snapping three times. I don't look at the photos right away. I put the phone down and kiss her hard, thanking her for letting me be obnoxious, thanking her for giving me what I wanted. All is forgiven as I climb towards the headboard and give her what *she* wanted; her face buried between my thighs (again, and again, and again).

On the way home in the cab, I look through the photos; in the first two she's rigid, you can tell I'm imposing, but in the last one we're both laughing and her face is radiant. I treasure it.

"Would you want to see me kiss someone else?" I ask, with obvious hesitation.

Her brow furrows. "No."

There's a too-long silence before she asks, "Would you want to see me kiss someone else?" I want to say no too, but it's a lie. I shamefully nod my head and hide my face in the pillows. She's surprised to hear this. She asks a few questions; I try and explain how the jealousy and fear mixes with lust and takes my head to strange places.

"I like watching you flirt, I like watching girls make eyes at you." It's hard to help her understand something I barely understand myself. She tries to laugh it off, but the truth is, it happens all the time. It's easy for her. She doesn't have to say a word and they just kinda flock to her. I harbor crushes for months before giving any signs, I err on the side of caution, I assume nobody's interested, I talk myself out of even a sure thing, but all she has to do is give a certain look, or rest her hand on their arm, and they'll follow her anywhere. She's strong and magnetic. She disagrees, but I know what I see. Our playful yet dangerous conversation has us both a little on edge.

She nudges me, kissing my neck and gripping my wrists with her hands. I pull them back, I love this game even though I know she'll win. I struggle joyfully, trying to break free of her grasp, she's stronger but I'm wiggly. I climb on top of her, straddling her as I pull my wrists away and switch my grip, grabbing her hands and fighting to pin them over her head. She flexes, her muscles giving me so much resistance as I use all of my might. I can feel her arms shaking a little, and when I manage to press her wrists all the way down to the mattress, I gasp, excited for a moment. Something about her smile gives her away. I squeal, "Did you let me win?"

She looks up at me and says innocently, "Girls like to win." My eyes widen, I can feel my blood pumping faster, but I can't tell if it's from the grappling or the conversation.

I bring my face closer to hers. "Is that right?" I ask. She looks down at my lips and back to my eyes and drawls, "Yes ma'am."

"What else do girls like?" I continue, starting to unbuckle her leather belt, not breaking eye contact. She thinks about it for a moment before answering. "Forearms." And then, "Freckles." I chuckle, suddenly feeling like a stereotype.

I start a trail of wet kisses down her stomach, stopping at that perfect ridge where her hips meet her abs, and say, "Girls also like these hip bones, don't they?" She's modest but she knows it's true. Does she know this is driving me crazy? Thinking of all the ways every woman who has had her before me has adored her makes my pussy throb. I want her in all the best ways.

My mouth moves between her legs, I breathe her in and sigh. "Oh," she says absentmindedly. "I thought of another thing girls like . . ." I stop what I'm doing and look up at her. "Gray hairs," she says, "and the younger they are, the more they like them." I'm paralyzed between her thighs. She said it so casually, but my stomach did a backflip thinking of all the beautiful young women who have run their hands through her short cut and fawned over those silvery highlights like I have. Does she know what she's doing to me? The cruelest sadist couldn't have shot a more accurate arrow, right into the bullseye of my favorite kink. She smiles, oblivious.

I want to say: "This hurts, stop. No wait, don't stop. Tell me about the last time that happened. Tell me her name, and where you met her. Tell me what you were doing when she noticed your gray hair . . . what did she say? Was she prettier than me? Did she love you?"

Instead I say: "Do they?"

I try to sound nonchalant. I put my tongue back to work and think of nothing else.

ON A HOT AND HUMID NIGHT

Mx. Nillin Lore

It never ceases to amaze me just how sexy they both are, and how lucky I am to even be there with them like this.

I'm supposed to be getting undressed too, but once my eyes fall upon Kate and Max stripping just feet away from me, their naked bodies illuminated by a single lamp in the corner of the bedroom, I can't help but take a moment to appreciate the view.

Kate gathers her long, dark brown hair over her left breast, positions the hair band from around her wrist down to her fingertips, then raises her elbows up beside her head as she tightly pulls her hair back. She puffs out her chest a little, arching her back, so that her already full, perky breasts lift in a way that makes it look like they've grown even more somehow. I feel my face warm from watching her. While seeing somebody put their hair into a ponytail may not be the sexiest thing that one might imagine about their partner, Kate somehow always managed to look so incredibly hot while doing it.

Of course, her being completely naked probably has more to do with it than anything else. With her hair now out of the way I let my eyes wander from her collarbone, which I so loved to kiss while we embraced, to her soft stomach, which I so loved to caress while I ate her out, to her thick dark pubic hair, which I so loved to run my fingers through whenever we played.

To my right, Max steps into their favorite black binder and starts sliding it up over their thick, powerful thighs, the same ones that always take my breath away when wrapped around me while they ride me. The tight fabric clings to their curvy hips, accentuating them perfectly. It's just a piece of clothing but I feel almost jealous of it, wishing that it was instead my hands clinging so firmly to their form. Finally, they take in a deep breath as they pull the binder over their chest. A smile fills their face and I know they feel so sexy right now, because they are, and that makes my heart beat a little faster, my blood pump a little harder.

Kate sees it too, she grins and smacks Max on the ass hard enough for the sound to echo off the bedroom walls. "You look fucking hot!" she says, and kisses them.

Max, in typical fashion, raises their arms up, their broad shoulders filling out instantaneously, then flexes their biceps for us.

"You fucking know it," they say, biting their lip and raising an eyebrow in that special little way that Kate and I both swoon over.

A huge smile crosses my face. It always fills me with happiness seeing how comfortable, carefree, and intimate with each other we've become. Over the past couple of years our friendship together has evolved into one that now includes a lot of casual nudity, affectionate cuddling, and, yeah, even sex.

When Max and I got married several years ago we knew that while we wanted to be committed to each other, that didn't change the fact that both of us were non-monogamous and polyamorous at heart. So, when our best friend Kate mentioned that she'd always wanted to experience a threesome, we jumped on that without hesitation.

The arrangement we have now is amazing. Max and I get our own apartment to ourselves where we can both live our gleefully queer lives as genderqueer, urban nudists, walking around naked all day, reading comics, having loud sex, and playing video games for hours on end. Meanwhile, Kate, who never wants to live with anybody else or get married herself, and kind of wants to murder anybody who stays with her for too long, is able to enjoy independent living in her own place while tending after her pet fish, loudly singing 90s R&B, and designing mansions in her favorite home decor mobile app games.

Then, whenever any of us desire extra company, cuddles, or ridiculously hot group sex, we're just a phone call and quick cab ride away from each other.

It's the absolute best case of friends with benefits any of us have ever had and now, after so many threesomes together trying out new positions, playing with toys, and learning how to make each other come the hardest, we were ready to get experimental.

Needless to say, this wasn't the first time that I've been naked with Max and Kate. What was a little different though was that we weren't getting changed together to go out for drinks or to a movie . . . no, this time we were getting ready to wander outside on a summer night in search of darkened places to positively fuck each other's brains out.

Lucky for us, Kate's apartment is in the middle of an area that's perfect for fooling around outdoors. While it's very residential, there were still plenty of moderately wooded parks, lots of trails, and a decent amount of unlit back alleys that would be very suitable for our needs under the cover of night. And we weren't going out unprepared, as just last night all three of us carefully picked out the large public park a few blocks away as our playground thanks to its lack of any substantial lighting and a really nice, full tree line surrounding the entire area.

With our location already set, outfits were the focus now.

We had put so much thought into the clothes now laid out on Kate's bed. Everything each of us wore needed to allow easy access to our most intimate parts, yet also be easy to cover back up with. That meant nothing too tight, heavy, awkward, or that needed to be buttoned or laced or tied. Everything had to be loose, light, and easy to undo, and do up, on the fly if required.

Max is already in the flowy, dark purple romper they had found at a thrift store just weeks before and Kate has her favorite gray hoodie on over her shoulders, not yet zipped up, as she steps into the pair of loose booty shorts I've lent her. I'd be lying if I said it didn't turn me the fuck on watching her pull them up over her hips, the fabric that has touched my girl cock so many times now resting against her pussy.

But I'm falling behind.

I quickly pull my shirt up over my head, letting it drop beside me, then start pulling my leggings down. I slow down a little because I know that Max and Kate will want to watch. They always do. It's cute that they try to hide it though. Neither fully turn their heads toward me but I can clearly see their eyes wander over to me just as the band of my leggings crosses my pubic mound, then over my semi-erect girl cock, causing it to bob a little between my legs before I bend over fully.

I *love* that something as uncomplicated as a girl cock springing out of a pair of leggings was enough to stir them both. In fact, I can see that it's working as Kate swallows hard and sighs while Max grins and looks me directly in the eyes. I haven't seen that wild, "I want to devour you," stare in a while.

"Dress please," I say, and hold my hand out.

It's in a bundle at the end of Kate's bed, next to Max, but they don't even acknowledge it's there. They're too busy looking past me. I feel Kate's breasts and stomach press against my back. I gasp as she wraps her arms around my naked body. One hand gently grabbing my testicles while the other rubs my chest and teases my nipple. Max walks towards me, grabs me by my hips and pulls themself close, kissing me before kissing Kate over my shoulder.

We haven't even left yet and I already know that tonight is going to be a good night.

Our desires for outdoor, exhibitionist, debauchery all started a few weeks ago, when Max and I were invited to our friend Jacob's weekend-long birthday party at a literal mansion just outside town.

This place was enormous. Built in the late 80s, it was three stories high, over 14,000 square feet, with eight bedrooms, five bathrooms, three hot tubs, a sauna, and a big indoor, saltwater pool, located in an equally rich neighborhood nestled alongside the river. Once a month, the impressive home would play host to a clothing and sex optional gathering for polyamorous, queer folks within the area and, after being invited many times by Jacob and his girlfriend Emily, Max and I finally decided to check things out for ourselves.

It was impressive that despite how many people were there, the building and grounds were so large and convolutedly designed, with rooms branching onto still more rooms like a maze, that you could always find a semi-secluded spot to tuck away for some fun. When we stumbled upon a balcony overhanging the spacious backyard, with an incredible view of the surrounding hills and river valley, a quick excited glance at each other was all it took to express what both of us desired.

Max sat down in a wide wicker chair and spread their legs apart, then pulled aside their shorts to show me their wet pussy. I quickly slid my cell phone from my pocket and opened the camera app, excited to watch Max put on one of their amazing masturbation shows for me out on that balcony, and to take photos to share with Kate as they did.

We were a little sad Kate couldn't be there with us, but she didn't really know the birthday boy or other guests like we did so it made sense why she didn't want to attend a potential sex party with all of those strangers. Max and I were a little different in that regard. The thought of complete strangers seeing us naked, maybe watching us fuck, was beyond exciting. It was desired. In fact, if the night had evolved into them riding me in a room surrounded by other individuals in the throes of passion, that would have been bliss for us.

Yet just because Kate wasn't feeling comfortable with being there herself, she still really wanted to participate. You see, while Kate isn't as much about being watched by others, she sure does love to do the watching. The thought of her two queerplatonic partners fucking for an audience, or being involved in an orgy, was exciting to her and she wanted to both see and hear all about what we were doing, as we were doing it, so that she could share in that pleasure in her own way.

Thank God for technology because that meant Kate could still have fun with us at the mansion from the comfort of her own bed.

So there I was, feeling myself grow, my girl cock lifting the fabric of my skirt ever so slightly, snapping photos of Max fingering their wet cunt and rubbing their clit. The warm summer sun beating down, a slight cool breeze flowing around us, as we tried our best to keep quiet enough to not alert any of the party guests who had suddenly wandered outside somewhere below us.

I did a quick little check around. Looking back through the sliding door we had came through, and over the edge of the wooden handrail surrounding us. Still nobody had noticed we were up there. I returned to Max just in time to watch them gasp, cover their own mouth with a dripping wet hand, and convulse in orgasmic pleasure. Once their legs had stopped shaking and they had licked their fingers clean, I showed them every picture I had taken, letting them pick out their favorites to pass on to Kate.

She responded in kind with compliments galore, and sent us an image of her middle finger hovering just above her clit with a visible string of come stretched between her labia and fingertip.

"You two make me so fucking wet. Give me more."

Believe me when I say that we gave her exactly what she wanted.

Over the course of the rest of the day we took every opportunity that we could to send Kate more photos and video of us teasing and playing with each other around the mansion. Quick shots of little things like Max flashing their tits in a random hallway, them holding my half erect girl cock in the garden outside, and me lifting up my skirt and pulling down my favorite pair of purple, lace panties to show off my fantastic ass while bent over the kitchen island. All moments captured sneakily as attendees were distracted in other areas of the house and Kate lustfully encouraged us by making requests for lewder and lewder things.

In one, Max playfully looked up from between my fuzzy thighs while I sat on the edge of the hot tub, their radiant eyes staring deep into the camera so that it felt like they were looking directly at me while taking me into their mouth. I decided to take a quick video clip highlighting my growing erection as they licked around the head of my girl cock, their glistening lips moving over my shaft, lapping up every drip of my pre-come along the way.

We had a lot of quickies that day, took a lot of photos, and as the sun set others seemed to get the same idea. Before long, Max and I weren't the only ones sneaking around to play. Be it moans coming from a locked bathroom door, or the rhythmic slapping of bare skin on bare skin coming from some unknown room tucked away from the rest of the festivities. Then there were the more explicit displays of deep dry humping, make-outs, caressing, stroking, and fingering amongst people in the pool, who all carried about socializing while pretending that they couldn't see what each other were doing under the surface of those near crystal clear waters.

Finally, late in the night, after most of the other guests had either gone home or retreated to their rooms so that everybody could compete for "who comes the loudest?", Max and I upped our game. This time they held the cell phone, its screen pointed at us both so that we could see Kate masturbating passionately over live video chat while I fucked them on the bottom steps of the large, marble stepped, spiraling staircase located right in the middle of the mansion to a chorus of sex coming from rooms all around us.

There, the three of us came together, arguably harder than we had ever come together before, and we vowed to take full advantage of the remaining summer months just like this.

Fast forward a couple weeks, and here we are on this hot and humid night. I'm already sweating before we leave and the park is still blocks away. Maybe it's the anticipation and excitement but the walk, though not actually that far, feels like it takes longer than I remember.

Yet despite all our excitement, once we're there we don't enter immediately. We circle it instead. Not once, but twice, carefully eyeing up the surprisingly dense wooded areas thoughtfully inlaid around the area.

I'm certain that we're being as ethical and considerate as we can be with something like this.

"Coming here this late was a good call," Kate says, confirming what we all feel.

"And that's why we're wearing what we're wearing. Nothing comes off all the way," reaffirms Max.

And with that, Max, Kate, and I finally enter the dense brush of the park and make our way through to a small clearing, right near a wooden storage shed we had spotted from our scouting efforts earlier.

Max is the first to make a move, letting out a lustful growl, striding over to Kate, grabbing her by the hips, pulling her firmly into their own body so briskly that it barely gives her enough time to let out a lustful moan, kissing her deeply. With Max's tongue still in her mouth, and her eyes closed, Kate reaches back into the dark for me. Her hand opens and closes frantically in search of anything that she can grab, moaning at her grasp on the neckline of my dress.

She yanks me over with such fervor that I almost trip into the two of them. Max is strong and firm though, and keeps us steady despite my stumbling entrance. The two stop kissing and Kate looks into my eyes. I can see the wet on her lips, glistening in the moonlight, and all I crave is to feel my own press against them.

I run one hand along the side of her face, up into her hair, then finally kiss her myself. It feels both electric and magnetic. So overwhelmingly good that I instinctively close my eyes to truly savor the moment.

It takes me a bit to realize that our huddled embrace has started to rock with some intensity I know isn't coming from any wind. I open my eyes to see Max's face, filled with pleasure, now cradled between Kate's neck and shoulder. Kate's hand is buried out of sight between their thick thighs, and I know that Max is lost in fucking her fingers. Kate smiles at me and reaches up under my dress too, finding my girl cock now dripping with pre-come, and moans as she uses it to lube up her palm around my pulsating head before she starts to firmly stroke me with her now wet fingers.

Max and I can't be the only ones feeling this good. I reach up under Kate's hoodie to caress her stomach, then slide my palm down under the band of her booty shorts. I quickly find her clit, already swollen, warm, hungry for my touch, and begin to stimulate her exactly how I know she loves it, before slowly working two of my fingers deep inside her.

Suddenly, the doors of a small church directly across the street from us fly open, sending what feels like an ungodly amount of light spilling into the streets and over the exact area of bush we're currently fucking in. The little building which looked so unassuming and quiet moments before is now alive with activity.

We all freeze, as if believing that's somehow going to make us invisible, but when I notice that Kate hasn't stopped stroking me I continue to curl and uncurl my fingers inside of her. After a few moments she covers her mouth and shudders, resting her head against mine as she tenses and convulses around me with such intensity that I can't help but push my palm even harder against her pubic mound and clit.

Max is less subtle. They bury their face back into Kate's neck and let out a muffled shriek as their legs quiver and shake, causing the nearby brush to rustle and a few twigs to snap. It's probably not enough to alert anyone, and logically I know that the trees and bushes are thick enough that nobody could see us without being right beside us, but we rush off behind the shed anyway, whispering expletives and doing our best to stifle nervous giggling as we move.

Kate falls back against it with a soft thud, her eyes wide in excitement, hair disheveled from the sweaty bush sex moments before. She cranes her neck to listen out for anybody coming to investigate, but the voices of those exiting the church trail off underneath the sounds of cars starting.

Multiple sets of bright headlights pour around the sides of the shed, cutting away at the bits of shadow keeping us out of sight behind it. They then dance about the rest of the park as each vehicle turns and travels off to the left or right of us, disappearing into the surrounding neighborhoods.

As quick as it started, we're back to it being just us again.

I see a single, thick bead of sweat trickle down Kate's neck and chest, tracing along her perky, left breast, catching a little glimmer of moonlight before disappearing fully into her hoodie.

I have to follow it. Reaching out I grab the zipper and pull it down in one fast motion, exposing her bare body to the night. She lets out a gasp, turning to face me just as I move to her side. Max does the same across from me and we immediately start to kiss, lick, and caress her heavy, inviting breasts and firm nipples.

We stay there for several moments, worshipping Kate's body with our own. Each taking turns to play with her hard clit, and to dip our fingertips into her warm, wet, messy pussy under her shorts.

I'm so lost in the moment that I don't even notice Kate and Max whispering to each other while I continue to play. Kate lets out a deep moan and straightens up, then re-positions me to take her place against the wall. They each grab the bottom of my dress and lift it up to just below my chest so that I am completely exposed from there down. I instinctively hold it in place so that they can drop to their knees.

Kate is first. With one hand on my thigh, squeezing affectionately, she grips my erection near the base, then slowly takes me into her mouth. Once I'm where she wants me she firmly closes her lips around my shaft, rests her tongue along the underside of my erection so that it perfectly overlaps my frenulum, and starts to suck and stroke me with long, smooth motions that send shivers of pleasure through my body.

If she really wanted to, she could make me come at literally any moment . . . but she doesn't.

Without saying so much as a word, Kate smiles lovingly at

Max, gives them a quick kiss, and shifts out of the way so that they can go to work.

Max ravenously begins to lick me all over. Running their tongue and wet lips along my erection first, teasing me with their warm breath, then briefly giving my sensitive testicles some attention by gently squeezing and tugging on them a few times. Once I've been positively slobbered over they take me into their mouth all the way to the back of their throat until they start to choke and gag, and pull my hand to the back of their head. There's no hesitation from me as I grab them and begin to throat fuck them the way they crave.

Like Kate, they could make me come in a matter of seconds, if they wanted . . . but they don't either.

Kate and Max pass me back and forth between them a couple of more times each, bringing me to the edge over and over again.

Finally, sensing I can't take any more stimulation, they both rest their heads on my thighs, my girl cock throbbing between their faces, while Kate starts jerking me, Max teasing my lady balls. This time they don't stop.

The orgasm is so incredible, so visceral, that it's almost beyond comprehension. Kate lets go of my girl cock and it starts twitching up and down with an intensity I haven't seen since my youth, thick streams of come launching feet away from us into the dark of night where none of us can see. Yet despite her best efforts to avoid the spray, Kate raises her hand to show me a big glob of my own semen dripping down her thumb.

"Ew! Clean up your mess," she says with a huge smirk on her face.

I grab her hand, licking and sucking the area completely clean of my come, and swallow it slowly so that I can feel it run over every taste bud along my tongue then down my throat.

This is going to be one hot summer.

WHATEVER I WANT, WHATEVER I SAY

Sinclair Sexsmith

"I'm going to do whatever I want."

By now, I have my hand over her mouth. My arm is pressed up against the plaster wall; the paint is scratchy and the plaster is cold. The curves of her—hips, ass, ribs—against my body are warm.

"And you're going to do whatever I say."

I'm not stupid. I know there are limits to what I can do with her. When I negotiated with her owner a few nights ago, we went over all kinds of things I could feasibly see myself doing, and some things that probably would never cross my mind. Although they did give me some good ideas, so perhaps I shall.

Her owner laughed when we started negotiating. "Honestly, I can't imagine anything you could do that would be over the line."

"That's very generous," I replied, smiling. I didn't want to take it as a dare, but it was hard not to. We laid out everything we could think of, and made it all clear.

She whimpers under the palm of my hand. Her hair is caught at my wrist, probably in my watchband. I might rip it if I move too quickly. I want to go slowly. I don't want her to rip; I want her to open. I lick my lips. She watches me. She keeps arching her back and rubbing her ass into my thighs. I wonder if she even notices she's doing that.

I reach under the loose, knee-length wrap dress to trace my way up her thighs. I savor the feeling of fishnets on my skin. The pads of my fingers fit perfectly into one of the little holes, and when I press just a little on her skin, I can feel how it dips inside of it. How easily I could hook my finger in, how easily I could tear away at the thin, delicate fabric.

Just pressing my fingers there is threat enough. She makes a sound that is half of a whimper and half of a moan, muffled by my hand. Her lips are open and she's almost sucking. I can feel her teeth. She won't bite me, though her jaw is a threat.

The straps of her garter belt are pulling at the raw top of her fishnets. I can feel the strain. They aren't going to last much longer. My breathing gets shallow and faster. I want to tear, rip, split apart, shatter. I want that moment when the pounding against her is what forces the sound from her mouth.

I did promise I wouldn't break her. It was a joke, at the time.

She isn't wearing panties underneath anymore. She handed them to me after she walked in the door, one hand on the door-frame to steady herself while she peeled them over her delicate T-strap heels. She knew the protocol.

I promised myself I would fuck her mouth before I touched her pussy, before I made her feel good. I promised myself I would focus on my pleasure and her service. But when I think about feeling her wetness on my fingers I feel the tension ratchet up and up and up. I want it. I want to feel her stretch open. I want to shove my fingers in her mouth with her juices all over them and feel her open her throat.

Slow, I tell myself. *Go slow.* The faintest finger on her velvet lips.

She whines. A sweet noise, a long high note from her throat.

"Shut up," I whisper. My lips touch her earlobe. "You're mine tonight. Just for tonight. Aren't you lucky, you little slut."

She swallows whatever cry was going to come out of her next.

I feel the folds of her. She is not bare; her hair is short and thin. It feels impossibly dry, and I try not to think about sinking my finger into the slick of her.

"What am I going to do with you, hm?" I slide my lips to her neck to kiss, to suck. To taste her skin, the sweat of her, and the sweet. She arches her neck, rolling her head back on my shoulder, offering herself up.

My fingers find it, the spot I was looking for, where she is pouring, where she is waiting for me. I wonder how long I can wait. I wonder how cliché it is to want to strap on and fuck her. I let her wetness coat the tip of my finger, but only that. I don't put it inside.

I pull it away, tighten my grip around her chest, and heave her toward the bed. She stumbles slightly and catches herself. I grab her ankles, one with each hand, pushing her up onto the bed and twisting her legs so she turns over onto her back. Her eyes flash a little fear, a lot of arousal. She bites her lip, unsure if she can speak yet, unsure if she can form words.

In a breath, I whip my belt from my jeans, slide the end back through the buckle, and loop it around her wrists. It'll do. I wrap the end in my fist, pull it above her head, and push between her thighs. She reaches for me. She looks at me, pleading. She wants.

I want to slide in. Her pussy is making a wet spot on my jeans. I want there to be something I can feel ready for her to take. I want the nerve endings. Instead, I have this: the color of my flesh, supple, flexible, on demand. I pull the buttons of my fly and they open, pop, pop, pop. It is easy to heave forward the swell of me.

She moans right away, with thick breaths and pressing hips,

and turns her head to bite her upper arm. Her lip catches and turns out. The pink of her is showing.

I rub the head against her cunt. Her hole is so slick it almost slides in just by touching. She is an invitation, an open door: come inside.

"Just because I'm going to fill you with come doesn't mean we're done tonight," I growl above her. She glances at me sideways, then lowers her eyes. She didn't think this would be it, did she?

"Yes, sir," she whispers. She steals a glance at me again to check my face and see if her words please me. "I will do whatever you say."

A place in my core liquefies and groans, filling a void that has needed soothing. That is what I need to hear.

I let go of the belt and stand. Is she trembling? Her wrap dress is a mess, falling off of her. I reach for one end of the fabric belt of it and tug, and the bow dissolves. One side of the dress spills back, exposing the skin of her stomach, the curves of her plush body, the curl of her breast.

"Open your legs."

Her face goes tight around her eyes, but she does. Her knees butterfly open and she slides her feet apart. My thighs are inside of hers, touching. I can feel the scrape of her tights when she moves. I want the indentation in my skin, want to feel the pinch and burn of it.

She has the expression of a woman who has readied herself to be entered. She knows she may or may not like it; she knows she may or may not come; she knows it isn't for her. She knows who it is for. She knows what she is for, and right now, she is a plaything her owner loaned out. She is a toy her owner is showing off.

"Pull your hands free of the belt. Open your lips." My mouth is going dry. "Show me."

She slowly brings her arms down from over her head and reaches for her pussy, spreading her fingers to show me what's underneath her layers. I grip her thighs with my hands. Strong. A handful. With the kind of pressure that will leave finger marks tomorrow. Gifts for my friend. She lets me push her thighs open further. I press forward with my hips. My cock is stiff in front of me and I find her hole with the tip of it. I keep my hands gripped on her thighs, the flesh of her giving under my hands. My fingertips feel the holes in the stockings again and I don't resist, I slide my fingers through them and pull. I slide my cock into her and push. She writhes and gasps. I flex and urge forward. The cells of her stockings burst with my pressure.

I slide in and out. My eyes are closed, I don't see her, but I do, through my touch, through the heat of her. I pull her thighs to me. I rip her stockings again. She cries out when it gives way. I feel myself close, so close.

"Please," she whispers. She has moved her hands out of the way so I can push in deeper. "Please."

Does she want it to end, or is she fearful of what comes next? Does she want my seed in her, or does she want me to pull out?

Doesn't matter. What I want is to flood deep inside of her. To surprise her with the pressure. To fill her. Instead, I empty myself, thrust after thrust, and she milks me, she catches me, she holds everything I give her.

My body thrums.

Then I breathe out. "Good," I say, righting myself again, pulling to my feet. Her dress is a piece of fabric. Her fishnets are shredded, falling off of her thighs. My lust is poured inside her and I can control myself, I can think, again. "Now that that's out of the way, let's start."

I button my jeans slowly and watch as she comes back together. I take my shirt off, bare from the waist up. I kiss her mouth and she is supple and so, so soft. Then I remind her, and I grip her throat, a little too hard. "Say it again," I tell her.

"You're going to do whatever you want," she whispers. She rubs her thighs together, presses her lips tight before swallowing. "And I'm going to do whatever you say."

I pick up the belt and fist it. I try to stop the wicked grin from spreading over my face.

"Oh," she says. "God."

PURE ENERGY

Giselle Renarde

I'd seen pictures of Angie before we ever met. I thought she was pretty. I didn't tell her husband, though. Not at the time. Even people in polyamorous relationships get jealous. Emotions spiral off in directions you don't want them to go. You try to maintain control over how you feel, but insecurity creeps in. Jealousy creeps in. Resentment. All these things. It can be overwhelming.

When I met James, I knew he was married. I knew their marriage was open. Angie had a condition that made sex painful, and she had a ton of baggage around it, so she basically told James to get his fill from other women. She just didn't want to hear about it.

I guess James sort of broke the mold, with me. He had some casual sex buddies when we met, but with us . . . well, it didn't stay casual for long. It didn't even *feel* casual. Right from the beginning, it didn't. There was a spark between us that wasn't purely physical. A metaphysical spark. It was emotional, it was intellection, it was spiritual.

And that spark extended in his wife's direction. Even before I met her, it did.

The first time I heard Angie's voice, it came as a real surprise. I picked up the phone one day, and there she was, shouting at me. At first, I couldn't figure out what she was saying, what she was accusing me of. I wondered if James had been lying when he'd told me they had an open marriage.

But no. That wasn't the case. Angie knew all about me.

That was the problem. She knew too much about me.

"My husband won't stop talking about you!" she said. "Caitlyn this, Caitlyn that! He knows he's not supposed to. He knows I don't want to hear about his other women. It's like he just can't help himself!"

"I'm sorry," I said, because I really felt awful that he'd broken the rules. Everyone involved in an open relationship needs to be on the same page if it's going to be a happy one. "Why don't we all get together and talk about it?"

That suggestion must have floored Angie, because she didn't respond right away. When she did, it was to ask, "What do you mean, *all get together*? You want to meet me?"

"Sure," I said. "I'd love to!"

She mumbled, "Nobody's ever wanted to meet me before. Not that I know of . . ."

"Well, I want to meet you," I said. "James says all kinds of nice things about you."

"He does?" She seemed blown away by the idea that her husband talked about her to a sex friend. "What kinds of things?"

Of course, once I tried to remember specifics, they all fell out of my brain. So I said the first thing that came to mind, which is that Angie had bought a new pair of red jeans and James thought her butt looked like a million bucks.

"He said that?" she stammered. "He never told me."

"Oh yeah. He went on and on about how pert your butt looks in those jeans, how they fit like a glove, what a great body you have . . ."

"Wow," she said. "I had no idea." After a moment, she asked, "And it didn't make you jealous, him talking about me like that?"

"No."

We'd been in my bed together, cuddling and chatting after sex, so I was in a good place physically and emotionally. I didn't share that info with Angie. I wasn't sure she needed the details. Although, what she did and didn't want to know needed to be her decision.

I told her, "When I've felt jealous and insecure in the past, it was often because I didn't know what was really going on. I imagined all sorts of scenarios that weren't based in reality. When I found out the truth, it always seemed so innocuous compared to what I'd invented in my mind."

After we'd chatted a little more, about nothing in particular, Angie invited me over for drinks. Except I don't drink—and neither does she, as it turns out—so she proposed smoothies instead, which was right up my alley. James would be drinking alone again. We had a laugh about that.

You'd think I'd be nervous about meeting the wife of someone I was sleeping with, but I was actually excited. I was more excited about seeing her than I was about seeing James, and James was no slouch in the sack. Our dates always got me pumped.

When Angie opened the door, I'm telling you, my heart skipped a beat. Honest-to-God skipped a beat. It wasn't just that she was pretty. I knew she was pretty from pictures on the internet. There was this energy around her that drew me in like a cyclone. Or am I thinking of tornadoes? Are they both the same thing? Whichever weather phenomenon I'm thinking of, it swept me off my feet and into her house.

The house she shared with James.

But James was nowhere to be seen. Just dainty little Angie with her pixie cuteness, her inviting smile, her shiny black hair, her Marie Kondo face.

And she'd worn the red jeans.

"James was right," I said as she turned to hang my jacket on a hook—I'd taken it off on the way over, because the afternoon had grown much hotter than I'd anticipated. "Right about the jeans. Your butt does look like a million bucks. Granted, I don't know what it looks like in other jeans. Or what it looks like out of jeans, for that matter."

Maybe I was more nervous than I thought. I couldn't stop yammering.

Angie didn't seem embarrassed, though. She just said, "Until you told me what James had said, I'd forgotten I even had a butt."

That made me laugh. As she led me into their quaint kitchen, I asked, "Where is James, anyway?"

She cocked her head. "Oh. He said he was going to call you. He got caught up at work. He'll be a little late."

I pulled my phone from my pocket. Sure enough, one missed call. "He must have phoned while I was on the subway."

In truth, I was glad to get some alone time with his wife. I wasn't sure why I wanted to be alone with her, or what I wanted to do, but the power of her presence drew me in even stronger than James ever had—and, trust me, the attraction between us was fierce.

Angie started pulling plastic food containers out of the fridge. They were full of fruits she'd obviously chopped up earlier in the day: watermelon, cantaloupe, sliced bananas, pitted cherries, peaches, pears, plums, apples, strawberries. The list went on.

"You didn't have to go to all this trouble," I told her.

Once the fruits were displayed on the breakfast table, she

started wringing her hands. "I had to do something. And once I started, I couldn't stop."

I reached for her hands to stop her wringing them, but she leapt away from me with such force she knocked one of the kitchen chairs against the wall. "Don't touch me!"

"I'm sorry," I said, and I really felt awful about it.

"I don't like being touched."

"I'm sorry," I repeated.

"It doesn't feel good."

"I'm truly very sorry. I didn't know. It won't happen again."

She calmed down a touch. Her hands fell to her sides. "James didn't tell you?"

"He told me some things, but not that. I didn't know it was an all-over aversion to touch."

"It is," she told me.

I apologized again. At first, when she smiled, I thought she was faking. I thought she just didn't want to make waves. But then she took a breath and I thought, *okay . . . we're good. We're really good.*

She asked me if I wanted to make my own smoothie, or if we should make one together. I opted for together. That way she couldn't poison me without poisoning herself too. I actually said that to her. She took it as a joke, I think. I meant it that way. Sort of.

We parked ourselves in the back garden, since the weather was fine. We hadn't had a lot of really nice days yet this year. When you get them, you want to take advantage.

Most of what we talked about had nothing to do with James. Nothing to do with anything, really. I think we were just feeling each other out, getting a sense of what this could be, what it could turn into.

She didn't seem upset with me, like she had been on the phone when she first called.

She didn't seem angry at all.

Once I'd finished my smoothie—which was delicious and boosted my mood as only fresh fruit can—I joined Angie on the padded swing where she was sitting. It had a bit of a canopy to block the sun, and I needed shade. You *can* have too much of a good thing, even springtime sunshine.

When I looked at her and she looked at me, I knew something was about to happen. With anyone else, I'd have known what that something would be. We'd have kissed. But with Angie, who didn't like to be touched, we'd have to try something a little different.

"There's a huge component to sex," I said, "that isn't physical. There's the energy behind it, the energy play, you know?"

"Oh, I know," she replied. Her voice wasn't light and airy as it had been before. Those words came out deep with desire. Deep desire. But it fluttered back to its normal register when she went on to say, "James doesn't know. He thinks sex is an in-and-out motion. I know there's more."

I nodded. "So much more."

Despite the freshness of spring, the air between us grew heavy, weighed down with craving. Angie had so much love to give, but her husband didn't know how to receive it.

I knew.

Or, at least, I knew I could figure it out.

I looked into her eyes. Black pools on marble white. But eyes are so much more than what we see. You don't go around touching a lover's eyes, but think how much you get from them, regardless. That was sex. Gazing into a lover's eyes—or, a potential lover's eyes. That was sex, too. No touching required.

When I shifted closer, Angie gasped. I wasn't going to touch her, and I told her so. She said that was a relief. She didn't want to touch.

"But you do want . . . this?" I asked.

"This? Yes. God, yes."

She closed her eyes. I watched her take in a big breath before closing mine too. Seeing her only in my mind's eye, I imagined what I'd do next, if we were touching each other. I wouldn't kiss her mouth first. I'd skip to her neck. I'd kiss her there.

When I imagined doing it, Angie let out a pleasured moan. "Feels so good."

"To me, it does, too."

No sense questioning how she could feel me kissing her when my lips weren't actually doing it. That was the mystery of sex, of connection. I imagined kissing her neck and she felt it.

I pictured myself moving down her body, kissing across her collarbone, unbuttoning her cardigan. My eyes opened a crack to watch her chest rise and fall. Oh, she knew I was imagining opening her top, pulling down the little white cups of her bra, planting my face between her breasts.

Licking one nipple, licking the other.

Sucking those sweet pink jewels.

I could practically feel her hands in my hair, even though she wasn't touching me and I wasn't touching her. Her breath grew ragged. What a turn-on that was. And yet, as much as I loved being touched, I was completely satisfied enjoying this sexual encounter with my lover's wife as an energy-only experience.

When I imagined working my tongue down her belly, that's when the whimpering began. Was it possible our astral bodies were actually engaging in the activities we imagined in our minds? Were we even imagining the same acts? Seemed improbable, and yet, when I imagined slipping her panties down her thighs and gently nudging her labia apart with my tongue, the sound that came out of her was like nothing I'd ever heard. So round with longing, so close to fulfilment.

I would get her there. I could do it without laying a finger on her skin.

Though I had no actual knowledge of what Angie's pussy looked like, my mind's eye saw it very clearly. Cute and sweet, just like her. So easy to lick, easy to savor. And the longer I imagined doing just that, the more she whimpered and squealed.

"Yes," she said, so softly the word was nearly lost on the gentle breeze of spring. And then she said it again, a little louder. "Yes." A little louder still. "Oh yes. Oh yes."

To an outside observer, we weren't doing anything at all. Just sitting together in the canopy's shade, rocking ever so slightly on the porch swing in James and Angie's back garden. But we knew better, just us two. We could feel the energy swirling. The tornado of lust sweeping us up. We wouldn't know where it might set us down until we landed. Would we even be able to find our way home?

Angie continued to whimper and whine as I spread my energy across hers, like grape jelly on peanut butter. A classic combination. Incredibly, all this imagining was satisfying in and of itself. There was an inherent satisfaction.

Picturing my face between her legs was so satisfying I didn't even want to do it, physically, if that makes sense. Maybe it doesn't. Or maybe it only makes sense to a select few. To others who realize great sex comes in many forms.

It comes and comes and comes!

Angie panted and purred, her breath just barely reaching my face. All it took was a thought, or a sequence of thoughts, and look at the reaction that thought provoked. Even unspoken, the idea could be shared. Shared between two people who'd only just met. But I guess that wasn't strictly true. We knew each other through James. He'd introduced us without even meaning to.

He left us alone, and look what happened. We made love in the back garden. We made love without removing a scrap of clothing. Without kissing, without touching. In spite of that, or possibly because of it, our energy play was some of the best sex I've had in all my life.

When Angie grew silent beside me, I opened my eyes. Hers were open already. We gazed at each other. Words were not necessary. I think we both knew we'd reached an incomparable level of love and devotion. After that day, it would never be just Angie and James or just James and me. The three of us would share a powerful attraction that couldn't be expressed. I didn't have words to describe it.

But that afternoon, in the sun-dappled garden, Angie suggested that when James got home from work we should all prepare dinner together. After we'd eaten, maybe we could retreat to the bedroom. Maybe she could watch us together. She'd be interested to find out precisely what it is we do.

THREE OPTIONS

Nicole Field

"Can I . . ." Angela cleared her throat, her voice husky. "Am I allowed to . . . kiss you?"

Steve's gaze considered Angela for a moment, before she slowly smiled. "Of course," she said, sounding like the very prospect of it delighted her.

Angela lifted herself up onto her knees from the floor, bracing herself on the seat of the couch until she settled beside Steve. Then she leaned closer, aware of Steve's every movement that brought her closer too. Angela's eyelids fluttered shut.

And then her lips touched Steve's. Soft, so soft, her lips parting against Steve's. The way they kissed was far gentler, almost reverent, than Angela would have expected. And she *had* thought of it, she realized. She'd thought about what it would be like to kiss Steve as she lay in bed some nights.

Steve's fingers worked their way back into Angela's hair, massaging at first, then gripping, gently but firm. Angela gasped under Steve's lips, and that sound made Steve chuckle. The hold of her hair loosened, and Angela was just starting to relax into the kiss again when her hair was gripped again, less gentle and firm this time.

"Steve," Angela gasped.

"'Miss', remember?" Steve corrected her. Her breath brushed against Angela's lips.

"Miss . . ." she sighed.

"Good girl," Steve said, before kissing her again.

It was as good as she'd imagined. No, it was better, so much better.

When Steve finally pulled back, Angela felt lips part as she gazed at Steve. Her eyes were probably fully dilated with lust. Steve's certainly were.

Steve cleared her throat before speaking again. "So, I take it we're not watching another movie?"

Angela bit her lip. She was unsure whether or not they were in a scene. "Um," she said, lowering her gaze experimentally. "If another movie is what you want, Miss . . ."

"Miss is quite happy not to watch a movie," Steve said with a smile. She placed her finger underneath Angela's chin and used it to lift her head, to draw her gaze back up to Steve's. "But I asked what *you* wanted, and I will have an answer."

Not daring to pull her chin away from Steve—and honestly not wanting to do it either—Angela hesitated, then said, "I would like to pay more attention to you than to a movie."

"That is quite fine." In fact, Steve looked incredibly happy with the prospect. Her eyes were glowing and her smile was wide. Still holding Angela's chin in place with her forefinger, Steve leaned in and took a kiss, which Angela gave gladly. "So, shall we move to my room?"

"Yes, Miss," Angela breathed.

Steve stood first. Angela waited until Steve turned back to her a second later, extending her hand out to her wordlessly. Smiling,

Angela took it, then allowed herself to be led back to Steve's bedroom.

"In the interests of good communication," Steve said, once they were sitting on the bed, both of them still holding hands, "I'm on the asexual spectrum. I don't really have sex."

Angela's mouth opened in a silent O of surprise. She didn't exactly know what to say to that.

Steve went on. "I *sometimes* have sex, but it's not often, and it's not the point of my play."

"But . . . kissing?" Angela found her voice again. "Kissing in the living room . . . ?"

"That was okay," Steve said. She grinned. "More than okay, actually."

Angela smiled, reassured that it was something that had been mutual. But there was still something else she needed to ask. "I'm not asexual," she said, looking at Steve, looking away, and then looking at her again. She wasn't sure whether her own sexual interest was something that was wanted; whether she should feel guilty for it or not. "Is that . . . going to be a problem?"

"I don't know," Steve said. "I've been with allosexual people before, if that's what you're asking. It's not automatically a problem. It just depends on what you want."

What she wanted. That was such a broad question, and Angela wasn't sure she could answer it right now.

"It's not something that has to be figured out right this minute," Steve reassured her, reaching out to touch Angela's lower lip lightly, instantly drawing Angela's attention back to her, and the present moment. Angela fought the urge to bite her bottom lip, not wanting to discourage Steve from touching her at all. "It's just something I wanted you to know."

"Then it's good to know," Angela said carefully, around Steve's finger on her lip.

Steve smiled. "You are so very good," she said.

"Thank you, Miss," Angela said, again carefully.

Steve's finger left her lip, and she gazed at Angela with consideration. "I'm going to give you several options for tonight, and I want you to pick one," she said.

To this, Angela nodded dumbly.

"One," Steve started, "more kissing. However, you can't touch any other part of me. Two, you can touch my body above the waist, anywhere you like, whether it's massages or kisses. However, you may not kiss my lips or anywhere on my face."

Angela gasped. Titillated, she already wondered how she was going to choose.

But Steve wasn't done yet. "Three, I have a great many small toys in the cabinet over there." Steve pointed and Angela followed her gaze to a small chest against the wall. "Same as option two: You can touch my body above the waist, anywhere you like, but if you use anything in that chest, you cannot touch me with your hands or any other body part. Only with the toys you see in that chest. And, no kissing my lips or anywhere on my face."

Angela looked from Steve towards the chest again. Curiosity got the better of her, and she asked, "Do I get to see what's in the chest first?"

Steve smirked. "No."

Angela had to wonder whether Steve had decided on that before or after Angela had asked the question. The smirk on her face didn't explicitly give away the answer either way.

She was definitely torn. She thought she could manage without kisses on lips or face as dictated in both options two and three. The toys interested her quite a bit. She didn't know if there would be another time that Steve would offer her free access to the box like this.

And yet, she knew she wanted to be able to touch Steve with her own hands for this first time.

That more or less cemented her decision. "Option two," she said.

Steve inclined her head, but chose to say nothing.

Angela took a deep breath in and let it out more slowly. "Can I please take off your shirt?"

"Please," Steve murmured with a smile as she lifted her hands from her sides.

Angela reached out slowly, reverently. This was the first time she would see Steve topless, regardless of the fact that Steve had already seen her that way. Angela unbuttoned the shirt from the bottom, revealing Steve's stomach inch by inch, and watching her face the whole time.

It occurred to Angela that she wanted to kiss Steve right then, and then her breathing hitched as she realized this was going to be harder than she had thought.

Instead of continuing to look at her, Angela's gaze lowered to the skin that had been exposed as she'd undone buttons. Steve's navel was bare and Angela realized that, even if she wasn't allowed to kiss Steve on the face or lips, she was still allowed to kiss her above the waist as per the negotiated rules.

"Would you please lie down, Miss?" Angela asked, her breath hitching halfway through the question.

"Of course," Steve said, lying down slowly.

Angela watched her stomach muscles move under the skin. She shuddered out a breath, then leaned forward and pressed her lips just beneath Steve's belly button. She immediately felt Steve's stomach ripple in response.

"That tickles," she offered in explanation.

"Oh, I'm sorry, Miss," Angela said. She wasn't, though. She wasn't sorry at all. Thankfully, Steve allowed her to get away with that small lie.

Angela moved next to kiss just above her navel, and again

another centimeter or so up. Her fingers were shaking when it came time to undo the next button, though she hoped Steve didn't notice.

Under Steve's top was a white sports bra. Angela was mindful to take care of that later. She didn't want to ruin this mood with any sudden movements, and kissing her way up Steve's stomach and chest were far too good to give up now.

Angela undid the last button of the shirt and then opened it wide so that Steve was exposed down to the waist, with the exception of the sports bra. Her light skin showed no sign of tan lines. Her navel was a small oval. Her clavicle jutted out beneath the skin. It was all so perfectly individual, so perfectly and specifically Steve.

"Like what you see, angel?" Steve asked her.

Angela flushed, not just to be caught staring, but at the sudden—new—pet name.

Steve caught it and tipped her head to the side. "Is it all right if I call you 'angel'?" she asked.

"I would like that, Miss," Angela said, smiling down at her.

Steve merely smiled back.

Angela's fingers trailed down Steve's chest, thinking about the sports bra and leaving Steve completely topless. Angela was so enjoying this permission to touch, enjoying the closeness between them. They were just two women sharing an intimate moment.

Okay, so maybe it *was* kind of sexual for her. Angela was trying to respect Steve, though, trying not to turn this into something Steve didn't want.

And so she didn't ask if she could take the sports bra off after all.

"Would you please roll over, Miss?" Angela asked, and Steve did. "Do you have any massage oil?"

She could hear the smirk in Steve's voice as she replied, "I do. It's in the box that you chose not to utilize."

It took a moment for Angela to understand what Steve was saying. "Wait, if I had picked that, I still would have gotten to touch you like this, so long as there was massage oil between you and my hands?" She felt affronted, and yet slightly impressed with how devious Steve had been.

Either way, she would have had the opportunity to put her hands on Steve tonight.

"Perhaps," Steve said, not answering her directly despite the fact that both of them knew what the answer really was.

Angela pouted, even though Steve wasn't looking at her, realizing again how she'd given up playing with the rest of the toys in that chest.

Still, this wasn't a terrible thing either: to be allowed to touch, massage, and kiss Steve all over.

She tried not to focus on Steve's perfectly shaped bottom, having deliberately not sat on it while she massaged Steve in a vain attempt to keep herself from thinking about how that part of Steve's body would feel under her. Certainly, she had decided against straddling Steve. Yet the thoughts now crept into her mind, almost as titillating as the feeling itself. Her imagination was good, and it taunted her with imagery of what might have been.

Angela's hands moved across Steve's shoulders and up her neck, towards the back of her head where she knew she, at least, kept a lot of tension. And it wasn't Steve's face, so she thought she was technically allowed to touch her here.

"Is this allowed, Miss?" she asked, wanting to make sure of it. Her voice sounded husky to her own ears.

Steve moaned her appreciative response, and that didn't help Angela's arousal either.

More and more, Angela could feel an insistent tugging between her legs, begging for attention.

"I should . . . I should probably think about heading home soon," she murmured, while Steve was still on her stomach and couldn't see the way Angela flushed red from the thoughts she was still trying to suppress.

"Oh?" Steve turned over until she was on her side, staring back up at Angela so she couldn't hide. "Are you sure?"

"I . . ." No. She wasn't sure. Angela wanted to stay here. She wanted . . . but the things she wanted weren't possible. Steve had told her that at the outset, and Angela really did respect that, even if her body didn't want her to right then.

Unexpectedly, a smile lifted the corners of Steve's mouth. "Do you want something else?" she asked, and she shouldn't have been allowed to sound so teasing.

Angela cleared her throat and tried not to think that way. "I respect that you're asexual," she said.

"Good. I'm glad of that," Steve said, pushing herself up to sitting with one arm. "But just because I have no interest in me having an orgasm, there's no reason why I can't get *you* off. If that's what you want?"

There was a question in Steve's voice, but Angela didn't know how the answer to that question could have been unclear.

It wasn't, she realized half a second later. Steve was teasing her again.

"*Yes*." The word found its way out of Angela's mouth, guttural, but sure. That was what she wanted. What she needed.

Steve didn't move immediately to fulfill that need, despite the offer, and it took a moment for Angela to push past her own arousal enough to see what Steve was waiting for.

"Yes . . . Miss." The words out of her mouth were more of a whine this second time, but she couldn't make herself regret it when she saw the way Steve's gaze heated, her lids low over her eyes as she gazed down at her. Angela was a tightly wound bundle of need. She *needed* exactly what Steve was offering her.

And then Steve gave it to her and, once again, it was better than Angela could ever have imagined.

BLOOD

Anita Cassidy

Tina places two fingers in her mouth, holds them there, sucking and licking them with her tongue. Wetted, she places them on herself and begins to move them over the insides of her thighs and towards the edges of her vulva, feeling along the folds and lines. This tracing is slow and teasing, the way she likes it. Almost every other finger that ever touched her here before has been a hasty one. Fingers that ferreted and poked, rather than caressed and stroked. Fingers and hands that had forced their way into her softness, rather than exploring and enjoying.

Out of her bedroom window, the sun and the moon hang among the thinning clouds. Angled against each other, one is lowering itself to the gently rounded horizon, while the other hangs, as patient as it is ancient, waiting for the sky around it to darken and then scatter-fill with stars.

As dusk slowly shifts to night, so Tina exaggerates the slowness of her own touch, giving herself more of what she has missed and longed for. Tonight, she is bleeding, and that only makes her more sensitive. Towel beneath her, enjoying her gentle fingers on the outside of herself, she feels for the wonder of female sensation, feels it across the lines of her pelvis, on her inner and upper thighs. She lies there imagining her clitoris as the bud of an extraordinary plant, one that has its delicate roots spread deep and wide across her lower half and which is nourished, not from the depth of her cunt, but from deep within her own mind, deep within her own self.

Using the heel of her hand, she presses against herself—one hand massages her thighs, the other fingers tease her lips as her palm presses gently down on her clit, pulsing up and down with a soft and growing pressure. Through the rhythmic movement, she listens to her breath, hears and feels the gasps as the pleasure begins to build, light flowing in a spiral upwards and outwards from her clit, teased on by the tracing of her fingers and the rocking pressure of her hand. Her breasts rise and fall, and she can feel herself about to come. Looking down, she smiles at her darkening brown nipples and she bucks her hips up against her hand, riding her palm, pressing down against it. With a gasp, her pleasure peaks and she cries out softly, "Yes!" Ecstasy ripples out from her center, through her body and back to the very fingertips that began it all. Sighing a little, she lies back against the bed and wonders whether to build on that one or just to be still and enjoy the shivering aftershocks.

Beep. Beep.

Her phone. It's a text from Shinoa. It's also typically short: *Can I come round? Xx*

Her reply is equally short, and immediate: *Yes please.*

Getting up, she pulls her discarded black underwear on and, with a glance in the full-length mirror, decides to stay in her T-shirt and stripy woolen socks. It's a look that suits an autumn evening and it's a look that also suits her. Curved thighs, soft belly, her creamy skin is marbled with pale blue veins. A constellation of blood and life.

As the kettle boils for coffee, she changes the towel on the bed, replacing it with a larger one. Shinoa will know what this means, she hopes.

Coffee drunk, Tina pokes about in the cupboard for biscuits and, eating one, she puts half a dozen on a small dish. Moments like this—the preparing of a drink and a treat—make her feel motherly, mostly because it's an act of small kindness that she rarely received from her own. Shinoa is only five years younger than Tina, but even that gap has brought out an unexpectedly nurturing side. The sex they've shared, along with all the little things they have in common—being only children, being enormous fans of Mass Effect, and almost anything '90s and sci-fi—has brought them close quickly, and that closeness has been a key that's unlocked a few doors in Tina's own understanding of herself. It's been both liberating and unsettling.

Her phone beeps. *I'm here.*

Tina picks up her keys and leaves the flat, going down the stairs to the front door. The stairs are lit by flickering strip lights and she feels a fleeting moment of anxiety about how she looks in this light, and of a neighbor seeing her in her T-shirt and socks. Shaking her head at herself, she wonders if this will ever pass, this anxiety about her appearance, this sense that her very importance is defined by how she looks.

Shinoa is jumping up to try and see through the window of the building's front door. The sight of her head bobbing up and down and the smile in her eyes makes Tina forget her anxiety and she runs, unselfconsciously, down the last flight of stairs.

Hugging and kissing in greeting, they walk back up the stairs, hand in hand, and into Tina's flat.

"I made co—"

"Shhh," Shinoa says, "in here!" and she tugs Tina towards the bedroom.

"Okay!" Tina replies, half laughing. "I so love that you want me straight away."

"Why do you think I got in touch? And after, we can curl up and watch a film."

Shinoa strips her jeans and jumper off. Her dark brown skin seems to glow from within. After turning on the night light, Tina pulls her own T-shirt up and off.

"Beautiful," Shinoa says, looking at her lover. Then, rolling onto her side, she notices the open window. "It's beautiful out there too."

The moon is pale and full; it casts an ethereal light into the room that feels almost solid, burnishing with silver all that it touches.

Shinoa lies back on the big towel, nestling her back into the cool cotton, her hips tilted upwards, black hair bushing out around her head in a beautiful kinked halo. Facing her, crouched between her open thighs, Tina strokes her legs, enjoying her scent. And then, leaning forward to kiss her, she puts her hand on Shinoa's hair, loving the way it feels both soft and coarse against her finger-tips. As she sits up again, heavy thighs curled beneath her, she sees there, on the lower hair, between the pink-brown skin of her lover's labia, a drop of blood.

"Are you bleeding?" she asks, softly.

"Yes," Shinoa whispers back.

"Me too."

"We've synced up."

They smile their shared delight.

"May I?" asks Tina, voice soft with hesitancy.

"May you what?"

"May I touch you anyway? I . . . I think I want to . . ."

There is a pause as they look at each other, eyes bright with shared understanding.

"Taste me?" asks Shinoa.

"Yes."

"Yes. Yes, you can taste me. And I want to taste you."

The women kiss again. The smiles on their lips make these kisses even sweeter. Tongues linked, taste each other's soft mouths. Shinoa gently bites down on Tina's lower lip and then, pulling back, says, "Go down on me, go down there and use that beautiful tongue on me. Remember you're safe here, we haven't done all this talking to not feel that now."

Tina nods, reassured, and, kissing Shinoa's cheek, tasting her speckled dark skin, she begins to kiss and stroke her way down the body before her. To feel care, to feel affection, and to know that she is safe: to touch and kiss, to trace dry fingertips on skin and over curves and rolls of softness, a softness which makes her want to bite and devour, enjoy and explore. This is sheer pleasure. Pressing her own heavy breasts against Shinoa's warm skin, feeling her sighs more than hearing them, Tina moves herself back up to her lover's ear and whispers, "First, I want to make you come, so I can taste that there, too."

Tina presses her hips onto Shinoa's, pelvis against pelvis, and they hold hands, fingers entwined as Tina gently grinds and rides her cunt against the other woman. Their clits bump together, the nerves and feelings across the whole of their sex respond, pressure and pleasure spreading in and back, out and down. Shinoa tilts up her chin and tongues Tina's breasts, a nipple held in her mouth which she pulls in, sucking hard, grazing it with her teeth as Tina gently bucks against her. No hardness is needed, just this mounting pressure, until they both feel their breath quickening and themselves coming close. Shinoa's head falls back to the pillow, her mouth open in a silent O, mirroring that of Tina's, as she too stretches her head back, her neck arched, and squeezing their hands together, gasping, they both come.

Tina holds herself there, fully in her body, every sensation experienced intensely. Then she slides her hands free, running them over Shinoa's waist and hips, over her round belly, which she kisses. And, while her own orgasm still echoes through her body, she moves further down. Wiggling her knees down the bed, feeling the warmth of Shinoa's thighs against her arms, she places her hands against those firm thighs and softly puts her lips to Shinoa's vulva, and kisses her there tenderly. Tina smells and tastes her lover, heady with the power of it. Teasing her tongue gently around the bud of Shinoa's clit, she then takes a smooth long and firm lick up, tasting the ripples of orgasm as they continue to vibrate through the flesh and muscle there.

Gently, helping the heightened sensitivity linger, but not over-doing it, she teases and traces her tongue all over, moaning slightly herself as she feels the rise of Shinoa's hips, feels the sensations she is causing in Shinoa's vibrations now.

Shinoa cries out with pleasure.

Sitting up, Tina sweeps her hair away from her face and says, "Now, I want to *taste* you." She places one hand on her lover's hip, wets her fingers with her own tongue, holding Shinoa's gaze as she does so, then, slowly, slowly, she slides her fingers gently up inside, stretching the lips apart, dipping inside.

Sliding her fingers up high, she can feel the blood is thick and warm. Pulling them out, carefully, she holds her bloodied fingers up against the moonlight. Dark and light-filled, she looks and wonders, conflicting feelings and thoughts flowing, and then—wanting only to know—comes the need to experience. Eyes closed, focused only on the blood, she places her fingers against her lips and tastes them with her tongue.

And in tasting she knows. Knows that this is also how she tastes.

"Together," whispers Shinoa.

Tina nods. She moves her legs over Shinoa's right thigh and they shift their bodies on the bed to create the moment together. The women lie side by side. They kiss, the still slightly bloodied fingers on Tina's right hand press against Shinoa's cheek. Their care for each other has created a space beyond shame, a place of pure love. Legs intertwined, breasts against each other, holding each other closer, they both nod their readiness and then slowly dip their fingers inside each other, and taste the traces of blood they discover. Metallic, and sweet. Night and day. Eyes locked on each other, fingers still touching and teasing each other, Tina's breath catches, her eyes bright with emotion.

Shinoa kisses her cheek. "Hey, what is it?"

"This. Your . . ." Tina hesitates, "*acceptance* of this. I remember telling my mum I'd got my period, and you know what she did?"

"Tell me."

"She looked away. Then she walked away."

"I'm so sorry," Shinoa says, and her eyes glisten.

The memory comes back to Tina knife-sharp and clear. But then it is replaced. She has a new association: this acceptance. Their shared tasting. The look. The smiles. The love.

"This changes me, too," Shinoa whispers back. "Fucking you changes me. Loving you changes me."

Tina smiles. "It's a re-weaving, an untying of knots."

They embrace, watching the moon fill the room and the night sky. The air is cold now, but, held deep inside each other's arms, they're filled with warmth and light.

A NIGHT OUT

Amanda N

These past two weeks have felt like an eternity. Now that you're here, I want your hands on me. I need to feel them on my skin, sliding across my stomach and around my waist. Unfortunately, it has to wait. Without thinking, you agreed we'd meet with friends.

We've just finished getting dressed and are almost ready to go. I'm wearing the burgundy boots you like and a little black dress I just got. Despite this, you sit there looking miserable, like you'd rather be doing other things.

When I come over to you I straddle one of your legs, pressing my knee gently into the crotch of your pants. I lean in and whisper in your ear.

"You should wear the strap out tonight."

I pull away and stand up. The look on your face has changed. You're excited!

"Why?" Trying to play dumb.

I just shrug my shoulders like I don't know. As I walk towards the door, I feel your eyes watching. I tell you I'll be in the car.

* * *

You don't want to be here. I can see it on your face and in your body language. The excitement from before seems to have left you. So I tell you it's too crowded, I need to get some air. Grabbing my bag, your hand in mine, we walk towards the car. The heels of my boots clicking along, while you're dragging your feet.

I push you against the side of the car and start to unbutton your pants.

You start to talk, stumbling over your words, "What . . . are . . ."

I bat my eyes, feigning innocence. "Well, you could open the door and get in so I can fuck you, or . . . we could just go back inside."

You reach behind you trying to find the handle. The look on your face is priceless and your composure seems to be slipping. I slide my arm around you and find the handle. When I pop the door you pull it open the rest of the way. Not needing any encouragement you slide across the back seat. I climb in behind you, locking the door as I close it, and dropping my bag to the floor.

"Pull your pants down."

Picking up your ass, you slide the pants down, just enough so I can ride you. I know what you want. You want it now and you want it fast. This is for you, and you know it. It makes you more excited.

As I move to straddle you, you pull my skirt up my thighs to my waist. It registers that I'm not wearing my panties.

You look shocked. "Where?"

"In my purse. Took them off when we got here." Nodding in the direction of my bag.

"You're awful!"

"You mean awfully good at fucking you, right?" I say as I slide your cock inside me.

You shut up and nod. I start slow, moving my hips against yours. Hands on my waist, your thumbs pushing into that soft spot near my hip bones. Every time you push the spot I moan. The harder you push the louder the moan. With my hands braced on the back seat I pick up the pace.

When I move my body the strap rubs your clit. Every time it hits the spot your body tenses just a little.

"Would you like to come?" I ask.

You nod yes.

I tell you, "I'm sorry, but I didn't hear that."

"Yes please."

So I move faster. My hips moving up and down, you hold my waist directing the pace. You move me quicker. Pushing your cock into me harder each time. I move one hand behind your head and with the other I lift your face to mine.

"Come for me."

You grab my hips and thrust yourself into me harder. As I moan I can feel your body tensing.

So I put my mouth to you ear. "Fuck me."

It tips you over an edge. The tension in your body comes undone. As you unravel, your moans are heavy and several "Oh gods!" escape.

I just smirk at you. "Better?"

"Yes dear."

"Good!"

As I climb off your lap, I pull my dress back into place. I gather my bag from the floor, and open the door before you can even pull up your pants.

"I'm going to put my panties on."

After I've put my panties on and freshened up, I go back out to the bar. If I want you to take control later, I have to toy with you a little. When I go to order a drink, I stand next to another woman.

Out of the corner of my eye, I see you come back inside. You see me at the bar and go to our table. As I wait for the bartender, I start a conversation with the woman. She's gorgeous. Short dark hair, dark eyes, tan with tattoos and maybe a head taller than me. As she talks to me she puts her hand on the small of my back. I can feel your eyes burning into me. Smiling and talking, we wait about five minutes for the drinks. When the bartender brings them, she pays. I thank her and walk back to the table.

When I sit down you're glaring at me.

"What?"

"You know what!"

I pretend to be offended. "I was just getting a drink."

"Finish it. We're leaving."

I try to protest but you just glare.

The whole ride back to the hotel you're silent and seething. I can't help but wonder if I pushed too far this time.

Once in the room you push me to the wall, my hands planted flat on the wall next to my chest. Your body presses against mine. My breathing is heavier. The places where you touch feel like they are on fire. You unzip the dress, your fingers tracing my spine as you go. Once you've pulled the zipper all the way down, you turn me to face you.

When I feel your lips on my skin, my body shivers. Slowly you kiss the top of one breast, then the other. Your mouth moves up my chest, kissing as you go. At my collarbone you slow, taking your time, prolonging it. Your hands move up my sides holding me a little firmer. From my collarbone you move to my neck. Then there is a bite. A moan I've been keeping back escapes and my hands tighten. My nails leaving tiny crescents. You grab the back of my head, pulling my mouth to yours. My body is humming. I can't catch my breath. You pull me away from the wall and walk me to the bed.

"Take off the dress."

I go to take off the boots and you tell me to leave them on. I do as I'm told.

You make me leave my bra and panties on too. Turning me to face the bed, you bend me over it. I hold myself up. My body is pulsing. My clit is throbbing. Standing behind me, you spread my legs. Slowly you move your hand between my thighs, teasing me. I arch, trying to get your fingers closer to my opening. You take it away so I can't have what I want.

"Face forward."

You walk away. I'm left bent over. Waiting is hard. Though if I don't, I won't get what I want. You lay your shirt on the end of the bed, near my hands. The smell of you is on it. It makes my body tingle, the scent of you has always turned me on.

When you come back you've brought a blindfold, restraints, and your pants slightly undone. The restraints are set to the side, teasing me. You slide the blindfold over my eyes and pull my panties down to my knees.

Your hand trails over the back of my legs. When you get to my ass you remove your hand. Seconds pass but they feel like minutes. Then without warning you smack one side and then the other. I let out a small yelp. My body tenses, and I start to feel the fire in my veins building.

To take away the sting you softly rub each side of my ass. As you softly rub, you ask, "Are you going to do it again?"

With the light touches, my body begins to relax a little. "Do what?"

Once again without warning you smack my backside. "You

know what you did." Your tone is patronizing and angry. "She bought you a drink and you let her touch you."

I don't get to answer. You start to spank me. Slow at first, one side then the other, with soft touching between each smack. Little by little you pick up the pace. The time between spanks shortens. I start to lose track of the cycle. My body tensing, relaxing, tensing, and relaxing. I can feel the wetness between my legs.

I whisper, "Please." You hear but pretend you don't. I try again, louder this time. You lean over me, pressing your body against mine, your hips against my ass. You pull my hair and your voice is like a growl in my ear.

"Please what?"

The words are on my lips but I can't make them move. You smack one side of my ass, now demanding, "Please what?"

The words are still stuck, so you smack the other side and a moan escapes. I ask, "Fuck me. Please fuck me."

Before I can say it again you grab my hips and thrust into me. Quick and hard. Again and again. Bring me close to the edge of orgasm and then you stop. I cry out a little, and you smack my ass and tell me to be quiet.

Then you push me onto the bed. Face down and still blindfolded, you press the weight of your body against me. It is your skin against mine. You move my arms above my head. Interlocking your fingers with mine, you hold my hands down. Your forearms press against mine, keeping me in my place.

As you hold me down, your voice is rough. "I touch you. I fuck you. You're mine!"

"Yes."

"Whose are you?"

"Yours."

"Who fucks you?"

"You."

"So are you going to pull a stunt like that again?"

"No."

You get off of me and move from the bed. You grab my hips and turn me facing up. You take off the boots and then use the restraints, tying me to something unseen. I feel you move from the bed, I hear you unzip your pants and them tossed to the side. When you return, you use your knee to spread my legs.

As your hand slides down me it slowly makes its way between my legs. Your thumb teases my clit as your other fingers tease my opening.

With your other hand you grab my hair again and force my head to one side, leaving one side of my neck exposed. You kiss your way down my neck, when you reach that soft spot between my neck and shoulder, you pull my hair harder and bite. At that same moment I feel you thrust two of your fingers inside me. I moan loudly as I feel you move inside me. My body is so tense I'm pulling against the restraints. You move harder and faster. As I get closer to coming you slide a third finger inside of me.

"Say it."

My breath catches and my body arches. You let go of my hair and grab my throat. Giving a small squeeze you demand I say it.

So I beg you. I beg, "Fuck me. Please fuck me."

My moaning begins to escalate. My body arches and pulls against the restraints. I move my hips against your fingers, feeling you move in and out. As you pick up the pace my voice is a whimper, "Please, please, please."

My pleas make you choke me a little harder. "Good girl!"

When my body releases the orgasm the whimper turns to a low scream of "Oh God!"

As you lay behind me you run your fingers through my hair and then to my neck. Your fingers trace the area where you bit.

A bruise is already forming. You try to apologize, but you don't mean it. You enjoy seeing your handiwork.

I turn to face you. "I have to tell you something."

Puzzled, you ask me what.

"I'm probably going to pull a stunt like that again."

THE SUPPLICANT

Michelle Osgood

The water is hot when you get in the shower. Too hot, maybe, but that's how you like it. Sharp and stinging, your skin already red and flushed with the heat. You immerse yourself in the spray, tilt your head back so the water can run steady fingers through your hair, loosening the curl into thick, wet lines.

You reach for the soap, a scentless, shapeless lump in its dish against the wall. These rituals come unthinking now. Your mind a soft buzzing blankness as you proceed to wash the smell of the world off you. The crowded train, the cubicle desk, the layers of foundation and powder and mascara that shape you into a pretty girl so you can move mostly unmolested through the world.

You rub the soap under your arms, through the soft thatches of hair you've carefully cultivated, a dykey secret under your pretty girl, professional girl blazers. You wash your cunt, your ass, fingers quick and perfunctory in each crevasse.

The water falls around you and the soap slides off. You make a lather in your hands, raise the foam to work it through your hair.

Once, twice. Rituals which are not followed have consequences, some more serious than others. You are committed to the thoroughness of this one.

And then you are done. Clean and wet and smelling only of yourself. You do not leave the shower. You stand under the spray and close your eyes. Your breathing slows. Water runs and runs over your skin, touches you everywhere. You wait.

When the invasion happened the first time, it was so shocking. So abrupt and unthinkable that your mind blanked. Left you with nothing but the pounding water and the vulnerability of your naked, flushed, scrubbed skin.

The blankness remains. There's a buzz to it now. A thrum of excitement, anticipation, along the edges of the empty space where the you who walked in the door, walked in the bathroom, walked off the train, used to be. She's not missing. She's waiting, too. You'll pick her up again on your way out.

The light dims. Your slowed breath catches. Every part of you alive with emptiness. Later you'll think of vessels, of hollow things created to be filled, of the holiness of a hole. The purity of not being.

Now you do not think. You only wait.

The shower curtain is pushed aside, and you see that one of the bathroom's light bulbs has been unscrewed. The harsh lighting gone soft in the light of a single bulb.

They step over the edge of the tub and pulls the curtain closed behind them. You can't see the lights anymore, the curtain obstructs your view, and your world is closed.

"You're so fucking hot," they say. They move towards you. Crowd in. They are shorter than you, objectively smaller in every sense, but despite the differences in your height you know they tower above you. They come so close that your bellies brush, soft warm flesh against soft warm flesh.

Your throat closes as they reach between you. One finger delves down through your pubic hair, into the cleft of your vulva, unerringly seeking your clit. They stroke you. Just that one finger. Stroking and stroking in one spot until you think you might die. Until you grasp at the slippery tiles to stay upright. Until you clench and gasp and shudder and say, "I'm coming."

They smirk and grab for your breast. Twisting and pulling your pink nipple. Grabbing handfuls of the flesh around them to bring them to their mouth where they suck and bite and you feel the pull between your unsteady legs.

They switch sides, assault the other breast. Use pain and sensation to bring your flesh to a peak. Rub and smack the swelling nub. Force a reaction and then punish you for it. You are blank and wet and have begun to mewl.

"Here." They produce a pair of clips. They fix one to your left nipple and heat blossoms, different and deeper than the heat of the water. They attach the other to your right. Your breath is coming fast now, your body arrowed down into three points: your breasts and your cunt.

The warmth of the water is too much now, slick and sickening. The air is heavy and panting with steam. You reach behind you and lower the intensity of the temperature. Again. Again. And again when that is still not enough. How could you have stood it before? Now you can barely stand, weak and faint against the destructive fire of your desire.

"Down," they order, and you're forced to the floor of the ceramic tub, awkward and hissing as you try to fit your limbs and knees into the space they've left for you while not bumping your breasts, which are caught and tender.

Water runs over your face. You blink and sputter, trapped under the spray, against the wall, by the tangle of your own gangly body. They take a fistful of your hair and drag your head back, force your face deeper into the spray. You cannot breathe. You cannot see. Between your legs your cunt splits open.

They hold you until you struggle. And then they hold you for a moment longer.

When they finally pull you free, you are shaking and gasping and unable to do anything but cling to their leg. Grateful for air, for sight. They have given you these things, you know.

The second your body relaxes against them, the second you are not fighting to fill your lungs, they pull you away. They shove you against the wall, the tile a cold shock against your back. "Open up," they command, and you are, you're obeying, you're eager, but they will not wait and shove their cock into your mouth the way they shoved you against the wall. Brutal, and before you were ready.

Your mouth floods with silicone like it floods with water, like your cunt floods with wetness. This is your favorite cock. Thick and skin-like and veined, with enough realistic give that you want to swallow the cock whole, feel it slide all the way down your throat into your belly. You have never worshiped a flesh cock the way you worship this. You prefer false gods.

You cannot move with finesse, trapped against the wall. You can only yield. Flatten your tongue, relax your throat, let your hands drop to the tub as your mouth is plundered. Your cunt clenches and whines and you moan as best you can with your mouth stretched wide and full.

"Fuck, fuck, fuck," they mutter, voice dark and low and barely audible over the pounding spray.

You close your eyes as they come. You let the heat and the dark swallow you, leave you dizzy and breathless. Their hips jerk a fading staccato rhythm until finally they pull back, withdrawing their cock from your throat.

The disappointment is immediate. You are bereft, abandoned,

discarded the moment your mouthed prayers make impact.

Your mouth stays open, tongue out, begging for a return. They reach down and your heart sings, throat greedy for fingers, but their hands move past your mouth and then they rip free a clip and you howl. They pinch the hurt flesh, rub it hard, twist, and yank as you sob and your cunt makes helpless thrusts against nothing.

They reach for your other nipple and you try to pull away, to shield your breast from the agony you know is coming. They grin and grab your throat, push their thumb under your chin and force your face back into the spray, and then they yank the second clip and you convulse. Pain and pleasure ripple across your body as your back bows, frantic to escape. They stroke over your swollen nipple, your skin so sensitive you can feel the rasp of each fingerprint ridge.

"Good girl," they tell you when you finally stop struggling. "Good girl," they coo when they let you free of the spray and you sag against their legs, trembling and clinging and abject.

"Now we are ready."

You nod. Your assent isn't required but you give it anyway. Nothing here is yours. But you give it anyway.

They fold themself down to the opposite side of the tub, leave the top half of you caught in the spray. You can't see, or speak, or breathe. They take your leg and spread you, sprawl your open legs across their lap. You are off balance and brace yourself against the tub. Blind and spitting out water with each breath.

They take the soap and slide it over your leg. Rubbing in circles, smoothing the lather up and down. You want to relax, but can't. You are too precarious without your sight, your breath, your balance.

None of which are yours. Not here. Not now.

They set down the soap and pick up a razor. You cannot see this but you know by the tightening of their hand around your ankle. You hold your breath, precious though it is under the spray, until the cold blade drags over your leg. You breathe again only when the blade lifts.

"I like you like this," they comment. You could ask what they mean, but you know: wrecked and wide and wanting. Caught off balance and trapped in the water and the heat. Bound by the spray stealing your sight and your breath. Swollen and flushed and begging to be filled.

The soap lathers and the razor glides, a rhythm you cannot settle into, not when they continue to manipulate your body, moving your limbs this way and that so you are forced to blindly, continually, readjust your weight. After each pass with the razor they slide their hand up, up, up, but never as far as you want it to go.

By the time they move on to your second leg, you are shaking. You are overcome by the effort it takes to hold yourself steady, to keep still under the threat of the blade.

As though they can read your mind: "I have been thinking about a straight razor."

You cannot shudder so instead you inhale, water pouring into your open mouth, warm where it spatters against your throat. Fear shot through with desire and your cunt is molten gold.

The razor curves up your calf. Your words spill out into the water. "I'm coming."

The blade doesn't waver against you, strokes steady through the lather. The image of a straight razor, the knife edge flat against your skin, coalesces into metal-sharp fear on the back of your tongue.

"Would you like that?" they ask.

You would. You wouldn't. You would.

Your cunt is a pulsing, greedy thing, undeterred by the thought of a sharper blade. Wet for them.

This time, when they slide their soap-slick fingers up your leg, they do not stop. They grip the dimpled flesh of your thigh. They dig in. Pry your legs wider until you are completely unbalanced and your cunt thrusts forward like an offering, soft and ripe. To be plucked and devoured, sticky juice dripping from hands and mouths.

The water is a curtain between you and them. Between you and your cunt. You are halved, two pieces, both belonging to them. Both pieces entirely under their power, their control.

They thrust three fingers into you, and become whole again. One body, one purpose. To take them and pull them deeper and hold them and keep them and take it and take it and take it.

"I'm coming." Your words are garbled and you are choking. Water pours across your face, your closed eyes, the wet mat of your hair. They fuck you deeper and deeper and the noises you make are lost in the spray.

"I think you would like that," they say, pausing only to put down the razor before they take both hands and peels your cunt lips open wide.

You're coming. You can't speak now, you can only gush, your hole clenching desperately at nothing. They pull you wider. Water cascades down the front of you, pours across your bared flesh. Your legs shake.

They fuck into you again and you come over their fingers, bursting open over their fist. They fuck you and your ragged prayers, *I'm coming, I'm coming, I'm coming*, are swallowed into the steam that billows between you both.

When they pull their fingers from your cunt and shove them into your mouth, thrusting your face up into the spray, filling your mouth with water, you start to cry. Your tears are hot even in the hot fall of water, salty and secret. Your chest heaves and your cunt thrusts and you come.

They withdraw and leave you crumpled at the bottom of the

tub. They give your legs a final pass with its hands, smoothing over you, pausing to make sure no hair is left. When they are satisfied, they stand.

"Come here."

You are sluggish to obey, heavy and sodden, but they are patient. When you are on your knees they take you by your hair and pull your head back. They slap you. Once, twice. Smack you roughly. You are swaying and liquid when they shove your face under the spray, and your stinging cheeks feel the heat of the water like another slap. They hold you under until you have gone limp, until your vision goes gray behind your closed eyes, until your cunt is a pool between your legs.

When they release you this time, they shut off the water. The abrupt change in sensation leaves you cold. You huddle in the corner, arms wrapped around your newly silky legs, your pulsing cunt the only heat.

They step out of the tub and dry themself off.

"I'll give you a minute," they tell you, not even looking in your direction. You swallow and nod. They throw a towel at you, disinterested in your cowering, and leaves for the bedroom. Your evening has only just begun.

Later, lovers who are not this lover will touch your smooth legs. They will admire your firm, hairless skin. They will come with your satin-soft legs wrapped around them, and think how pretty and femme and feminine you are. They will appreciate your attention to detail, your consideration for their comfort. And you will smile a secret smile and sweetly say, "You're welcome," and no word of this ritual will cross your lips.

TORRENT AND TUMULT:
A BIPOLAR ROMANCE

June Amelia Rose

My Mistress wasn't letting me come for a whole week.

She had locked me in chastity many times before. I was the one who had first asked her to. I craved the way she'd take control of my orgasms, deal them out to me, make me beg, deny them just when she felt like fucking with me, because watching me squirm as I was frustrated and not allowed to come turned her on so much.

But it was always for a day or two. This would be the first time I was locked up for an extended period of time. My clit belonged to her. The small pink metal cage would stay with me at work, through all my dinners and dates with other partners, while I slept and showered.

The excitement was unbearable, and heavenly. I spent my days turned on from how hot it was to be locked up for so long, frustrated it wasn't sooner but knowing it was for my own good. I couldn't wait. I anticipated what she had prepared for me, what lovely prize awaited my greedy little submissive heart.

And finally, day seven came.

* * *

My body has an addiction to the swings of tumultuous emotions.

You were born with rivers of fire inside you, my mother said to me once, during a crying fit while I was trying to bite my own tongue out of my mouth. *You have the strength and the sadness to be calm, you have the drive to accomplish anything.* She didn't know then how apt those words would become, on the eve of my diagnosis twenty years later, when the key clicked into the lock as my therapist spoke the litany to me in a divine tongue. Bipolar I, with features of mixed episodes, rapid cycling, and melancholia. They unfurled like the secrets of my family's jewelry chest, a genetically rich inheritance of chemical imbalance cooked up in a pressure cooker of psychological trauma.

Torrent and tumult, then calm drops on a drooping, dying lotus flower. That was how I lived for most of my life. I would stir and then still, I would start and then freeze. Emotions were like another language to me. I was a foreigner to emotional stability.

You can only live for so many years with a deficiency in relating to other people until other people's lives start to blow up too. I think I lost every friend and every relationship I've ever had, all to a mood spoken in words I didn't understand. At a certain point, a change needs to come. The way out is through.

When we first met in the rooms, I knew she had come from where I had.

Alcoholics Anonymous is just like that. Instantly you just have a connection with people because they think like you do, they've been through what you have, they've seen the bottoms of the gutters and sewers you've spent years trying to get out of.

Even if you have nothing in common socially, no hobbies, a completely different worldview, none of it matters in the rooms. The fellowship of it all smooths over everything.

In those first days I tried to embrace the hug of the chalky decaf coffee. I always had to take it black because most alcoholics in the rooms won't think ahead to stock soy milk.

"Hi, I'm Melody, I'm an alcoholic," I would say, my voice flat and nervous and wanting. There's a certain ego death that comes with announcing your ailments to the other members of your special class.

The meeting that she sat next to me, the trans women's meeting up over on the church on Nostrand and Willoughby, I knew I'd seen her before. The domme who everyone said was too much chaotic energy.

Her hair was a searing blonde.

Sage used to be a bassist in a punk band nobody's ever heard of, and she roadied for a few years for a punk band everybody has heard of.

During her share in the meeting that night, she mentioned bipolar disorder and punk rock.

I went up to her afterwards.

"Hey, can I have your number?" I asked her. I'm normally not forward about that kind of thing, but the moment was too good to be passed up. It needed to be seized.

"Sure," she said as she typed her number into my phone.

"I just want you to know, it's kind of a, more than fellowship thing."

"Oh, I think I've seen you around the scene before," she said, her face puzzling out a plan. "Never knew you were one of us." She looked down at my faux-leather bondage cuff. "I can think of some uses for you."

I was in charge of cleaning her house, doing her laundry, washing her lingerie. All these chores that she delegated so matter of fact.

After so many years of alcoholism, poisoning a self I didn't care about, it was helpful to throw myself into caring for someone else. My hands worked for her with so much intention.

I got pleasure and guidance out of serving her. One time, while she was beating me with her custom wooden pink "Mistress" paddle, with spikes on one end, she barked at me.

"You love serving me, don't you?"

"Yes Mistress! I love to serve! I love following your orders!"

Whack.

"You already do anything I want," she said. "Because I own you."

"Yes Mistress!" She turned the paddle on its side and dug the edge into the beginnings of a purple bruise, already beginning to break across my ass like sunlight.

"Hahhh," I cried.

"You do it because it pleases me, don't you?" she said.

"Yes Mistress!" I cried out. "Nothing pleases me more."

She flipped the paddle over to the spiked side, a masochistic reward for answering so well.

With a stroke of love she swiped the paddle against me, my ass splattering a rain of blood across the wall and down her face.

Thank god I just got tested, I thought to myself.

She licked a drip of blood off her upper lip.

"You're welcome."

I tried my best not to use my service to her as a substitute for a sense of self, but I worried I wasn't always completely living up to that. She assured me it was fine, but the past had me by the throat.

My ex-girlfriend was this famous punk tattoo artist, a bohemian goddess. Mabel Connolly had straight pink hair. We didn't talk about her much. An ex-domme is a curious presence. She looms over, incessantly, because she too once owned just the same. The lasting marks of ownership run deep.

Our days together were chaotic. Looking back, they read like a drop of blood, blotting like ink onto a tissue. The intensity rippled outward. It was an unsustainable truth, collapsing in on itself. We tried to fix all our problems. They were wantonly accidental cuts from a straight razor, stopped up and plugged with our little compromises.

My arms are filled with the needle-stroke scars she gifted to me. A whole tattoo sleeve sliced up with little memoirs drawn by her hand. I carry them with me, to look at and hate when I'm depressed and to bring me great joy when I remember all the good times we had. The little heart that said "Woe" in gothic type. The dyke tattoo we got together.

Our falling out was a psychotic break for me that led to my first manic episode. I stayed up for seven days straight, reading books into the hours of the morning. I would try to get some sleep but there was still so much to *do*. If she could leave me, everything else would. And time was definitely leaving me, infinitely. It seemed like the only thing that couldn't leave me was death. And no, I don't mean that in the gothic glamor way, I mean it in the Camus suicide type way. Cutting yourself to feel alive type way.

It was a sunlight of dread burning behind my eyes.

Liquid gold emotions welled up with the burning embarrassment of all my failures. I couldn't focus, I couldn't sleep, I couldn't concentrate at work. I would leave my desk to cry in the bathroom and then come back into my seat laughing about how beautiful the hurt of life was. When eating I would forget how to hone my muscles on chewing. It seemed so pointless. Food was a means to an un-end and I wanted a means to an end. That led me to the razor, and the first time I've ever cut for self-hatred. A rain of not loving masochism, but self-hatred (there is a vast difference), that had crossed into active destruction. It was the only way to let my gilded despair out.

And then one thing led to another, and another and another

and they all came at once in my mind, lofty ideas crashing, punching into each other. Then all those things led to one more thing and I woke up in the psych ward, and that was what led to them knighting me with the noble cause of Bipolar I, with mixed features, rapid cycling, and melancholia. It was a litany of a diagnosis I would learn to recite quite well over the next few years, a roll call of the hurt that exists in the memories of my brain's pain-body.

It is so helpful to date and serve someone who knows how beautiful and vivid everything is, how imperative every action becomes in the moment, how simple transactions like how many sugars to put in your tea are indicators of life and death. At the same time, two bipolar people dating is the equivalent of two boiling kettles fucking each other.

I often think about the extremes of kink, and the highs and lows that go along with them. Can someone who has manic and depressive episodes even engage in kink safely? For a while, I doubted myself. I was an intense person with intense emotions purposefully playing with intense sensations. I was afraid I was purposefully putting myself into situations that spiked my intense moods.

But kink can be a healing practice. It reintegrates your body and mind together with the expressions of love and emotions. I realized that when I engaged in BDSM, I was reconnecting with the parts of myself that I thought I'd lost forever. I was becoming one and whole with my desires, with the universe, with my partners. And that was when true healing began.

I think the first pillar in all of this is self care, knowing that you are keeping the tumultuous aspects of your life under control. For years I didn't do that, and in many ways I was practicing unsafe kink. I was being unfair to myself, and unfair to my partners by extension.

Sage took two pink lithium pills every night. A little pink salt that went so far it re-organized the inner fabrics of her brain. Lithium works best for people with hugely manic episodes. Me, I was on depakote, the couch potato cousin of lithium. Better for people with a rounded out episodic nature.

I've never seen Sage during a major bipolar episode, but from what she's told me, hers are classic strung out mania, and then the downturn of an abyss of depression and suicidal, nihilistic ideation. One time roadieing for Rancid she quit in the middle of nowhere in West Texas. She refused to get in the van. She was convinced they were all actually cops. The friends she'd grown up with at Gilman in the Bay for years.

So after a few hours of trying to convince her, they left her.

Of course they didn't actually leave her. They drove out of sight down the road and called 911 and told them their bipolar friend was off her meds and in the midst of a manic episode on the side of the highway in the middle of the desert. It took the ambulance four hours to arrive. Luckily, even though she was trying to hitchhike, no one picked Sage up.

She spent three weeks at a hospital in Texas. Her paintings from then are these vivid collages of punk stencils and words and sayings, all less than one centimeter tall, filling up page after page of computer paper. If you've ever used one of the bendy pens they give you in the psych ward, her neurotically legible calligraphy was a legendary achievement to be chronicled in the scriptures of zines for years. The woman was actually convinced she was the simultaneous reincarnation of Nick Blinko and David King, neither of whom were dead yet.

Of course, the band let her back into the road crew when she got out, after a few conversations and assurances. They made her promise to take her diagnosis seriously, and forbid her from drinking or doing drugs for the rest of the tour. Sage agreed. I can't imagine what it must've been like to have detoxed from alcohol dependency in the back of a van with a bunch of sweaty dudes, all of whom were drinking.

Bless her, she did it. Besides the few lapses in medication and more manageable episodes, she kept on that promise. She says it makes her domination better.

She did have a relapse. In 2014 she got bottom surgery, and the painkillers they put her on were remarkably seductive. It scratched an itch in her she didn't know she had. The next year, her dog died. To cope, she started drinking again, figuring she could but obviously she couldn't. That relapse led her into the rooms for the first time.

And that was her, my bipolar Mistress.

"You've been my little good girl. Mistress is pleased."

I kneeled on that floor for her, obedient and waiting on the faux-fur carpet as I gleamed under the sheen of my glittering accomplishments. My expression shined with pride. My Mistress was happy with me.

"Here's your reward. You are going to pleasure me."

My heart dropped into the pit of the gutter of submission, a reminder that I was hers and she was my owner. The sweet roses of her touch against my ear, brushing my hair back as she spoke, they lit the candle inside me. I was ready to serve.

She leaned into my ear, whispering with a voice that ensnared me like thick syrupy quicksand. I was hers.

"You are going to touch me in every way I say."

I nodded my head.

"What do you say?"

"Thank you, Mistress."

"Thank you for what?"

"Thank you for the opportunity to serve you," I said.

"And?"

"Thank you for locking me in chastity and giving me the privilege of controlling my orgasms."

"You're welcome. Do you want to come tonight?" she asked.

"Please Mistress, please. I've been a good girl, I've done everything you've said."

"Beg a little harder," she said.

"I . . . I don't know how."

"Then I guess you won't get to come," she said, matter of fact.

I cried out loud at the thought, my thighs shifting and rubbing between themselves to relieve some of the tension.

"Get down," she commanded. I dropped down, my forehead an inch from the floor.

"Ask my feet if you are allowed to come."

"I . . ."

I stared at her toes, a subtle chipped black polish that I'd painted for her as an act of service only a week before. *A treat for you,* she'd told me. She knew this was my weak spot. She knew it would make it harder for me to concentrate, and she wanted that.

"Please let me come," I cried out.

I heard her silence contemplate the notion.

"No," she said. So stern and simple. "So, where were we? You are going to pleasure my pussy in all the ways I ask."

I nodded. I was too frustrated to form words.

"And me?" she purred. I could feel the shape of her voice curl into a grin. "I'm not going to touch you at all." My muscles clenched. Pure elation, elevation, ecstasy.

"This is about me and my pleasure. You don't get any unless I say."

I leaned into her clit as she spread her legs. The scent was everything I always dreamed about when I used my vibrator in bed, fantasizing about pussy. Most of the time, the pussy I envisioned was hers.

She got a kick out of that.

I brought my tongue out soft and stroked her clit, then the outside of her labia, up and down and around and then back up again to her clit, which I knew she liked the best. I lapped not like a dog but like a delicate, obedient, pocket-sized puppy, with precision and tact.

"Hand, inside," she commanded without even looking at me, her voice electrified by the symphony of my tongue. I started with two fingers.

"More," she commanded. I went up to three, moving in and out around my long femme nails. Her pussy juices lubricated well, but I grabbed some lube from her nightstand to add a bit more. My tongue kept working away at pleasing my Mistress.

The torrent of emotions, the thrashing of my womanhood welled up against the insides of my chest. My nipples were erect. Sage kept pinching them between her black toenails. She twisted and pulled as I moaned in heat, my clit pressing up against the inside of the chastity cage.

I got my fourth finger into her. My long red nails looked especially tantalizing dipping in and out of her. I'll never forget the butch at work who had told me all lesbians have short nails, and I thought to myself, *Not if you've seen the dykes I hang out with.* Femme fingering is its own special power.

"I dilated every day for five years to be able to fit a fist in," Sage said. "Don't think you'll be able to fill that much on your first try."

I licked and I licked as her pussy juices flowed out and over onto the bedspread. My fingers continued to move as I subtly bucked them up towards her clit every now and then as she writhed in pleasure. Her grip on my hair turned violent and sexy.

I kept rubbing my thighs together, shaking my chastity cage for an itch I wasn't allowed to scratch.

"My . . . little . . . slut!" she shouted as she came, her muscles clenching against my face. The breath was released from the air, and everything stood still. She had channeled her own pleasure into the obedience of the world, the elements, the universe. I was enraptured at how much I cared for her.

"Okay, now you know what to do. Go get some cleaning supplies and clean the come off my bedspread. I don't want it staining."

After cleaning the come off of the bed, I stood before her sprawled out in bed, waiting for a command. I tried not to gesture towards my chastity device, but it was all I could think about.

"Maybe next week," she said.

"My clit is yours, Mistress. Whatever you say."

"You don't want to beg?"

"Of course I do. But I'm so happy right now. This is the life I've always dreamed about living, and it isn't in a story or a promise in the future. It's here, and it's now."

"Mistress is here with you."

"I love you, Sage," I said, breaking character a bit.

"I love you too, Melody."

We slept together, me wrapped in a childish embrace around her naked body, the body I spent most of my days worshipping. It felt like home. With my Mistress next to me, all the tumultuous emotions didn't seem so bad. They were far off, like raindrops on a distant planet I knew I would be able to overcome.

That night, my lotus flower bloomed.

THE ONE PENIS POLICY

Tobi Hill-Meyer

There was just something about being desired. It'd be great to have something more serious, but sometimes just touch can make such a difference. Celia found touch an intoxicating balm for all her anxieties and fears in the world. But because of its scarcity, she told herself, sometimes that means making compromises. This wasn't the first time she was hooking up with someone primarily for the sex.

In this case, she had found Shannon on some new lesbian dating app. For some reason, the lesbian apps always have so many people not actually looking to hook up. Even more of them nervous of the idea of hooking up with a trans woman. Celia couldn't afford to be picky.

When they first met, Shannon asked to take a selfie together, only afterward explaining her phone was set up to auto-upload to a shared cloud account with her husband. Shannon explained it was for safety. "You never can be too careful with internet dating."

Celia found it off-putting that some man she's never met was now looking at her photo. On top of that, talking about her husband within the first thirty seconds of meeting was a bad sign. She was on a lesbian app, so Celia knew she wasn't straight, but that was the first of several things that evening that felt straight about her.

It became clear that she was pretty well-off—a kind of wealth uncommon in Celia's community. On top of that, most of Shannon's friends and community were straight, and the few queer friends she had also were cis women married to men. And while Celia wouldn't be able to explain why, there was something about her small talk that just felt like how straight people talk. The only thing about her that might make Mike Pence nervous was that she was a slam poet. That and, of course, the sex with women thing.

There are all kinds in the wide LGBTQ spectrum, but this posed a particular concern for Celia. It wasn't judgment or any kind of queer purity test. If most of Shannon's sexual experience was with men, there was a risk she might see Celia's body and try the same techniques she was used to using on cis men's bodies. Before they had left the coffee shop, Celia had resolved that if they did have sex on this first date, she would leave her underwear on.

Shannon had a similar concern. She hadn't known many trans women, and certainly hadn't had a relationship with any. But when they matched she told herself that it didn't matter. She didn't want to let bigotry influence her and refused to let the fact that Celia was trans lead her to treat her any differently. And to show she held no prejudice here, she kept finding moments in their conversation to make it clear she saw Celia as a woman.

She started with, "It's so nice to be on a date with a woman" and followed it up with, "I haven't had a chance to hook up with another woman in years." She felt proud of herself when she worked in "women, women like us," despite being unaware of how that phrasing is used in trans spaces. She thought it might be good to mention that since she's into men as well there's no need to worry how she'll be around the genital thing, but she couldn't find any opportunities to say something like that that didn't seem crass.

Celia noticed that for each one of these instances, Shannon was in fact acting in a way that she wouldn't with cis women. She was overcompensating in a way that made it clear that being around a trans woman was an unusual situation for her. Nonetheless, Celia did find it reassuring to know she was trying and that this wasn't a bi-curious experiment or "best of both worlds" situation.

After the coffee shop, they went on a walk. Both women were nervous to make the first move, and the longer time went on both women feared the lack of any action so far meant this date was a bust.

When Celia got up the nerve to initiate a kiss, it was like a dam broke. Suddenly Shannon's hands were all over her. One hand was wrapped around her side. The other on the back of her neck. When their lips parted, Celia let out an audible gasp. Shannon grinned. Any doubt either of them had was gone. They quickly headed back to Celia's place, not too far from where they were walking.

Back in her bed, Shannon was writhing against her, trying to get as much touch as possible. Celia wrapped her hands around Shannon's hips, pulling her closer. Shannon was careful to avoid touching Celia's body in any way that might not be okay, but it made Celia worry it was a sign she didn't want to go any further.

Instead, Celia guided her thigh between Shannon's legs and pushed upward. Shannon moaned, clenched her legs around Celia, and kissed her deeply. Celia ground herself into Shannon's thigh. Gripping and pulling they pressed into each other. Celia ran her lips softly over Shannon's neck and then she was suddenly coming. Celia had a flash of jealousy for how easy it seemed to be for Shannon to orgasm, considering it was much more difficult for her, but resolved to take full advantage of the situation. She didn't come herself, but brought Shannon to orgasm twice more before they ended for the night.

Afterwards, when Celia was reflecting on the date, she thought about how Shannon wasn't exactly who she was looking for, but the sex had been pretty good, and despite the awkward moments she realized there's no way the sex would have been that good if she hadn't genuinely liked Shannon. Celia even thought her poetry was good. Or at least not bad.

The second time they met, Shannon invited Celia over to her place and it quickly became apparent there was no way poetry money paid the rent. It was hard for Celia to tamp down a feeling of resentment. She knew the luxuries in Shannon's home were possible because of the kind of stability that having a primary partner you're building a life with allotted—especially one not subject to the wage gap.

Some of the folks Celia had dated had really genuinely cared about her, but none of them would ever have thought of moving in. And when she thought of it, at least half of them already had partners they lived with—there was no way to fit her into their life like that.

Shannon mentioned that they should wrap things up by eight because her husband would be home around then. Celia reminded herself this is exactly why she wanted someone just to hook up with. She could deal with being single. She had friends to rely on. Friends who she shared her fears and concerns with, who took care of her when she was sick, who helped out when she was in between jobs. She didn't need a partner for all of that. In fact, it can be worse to look for it, get your hopes up, and constantly be turned down. But she didn't want a life of celibacy.

With so little time, they got right down to business. They were still in the kitchen when Shannon took hold of Celia's hand and guided it down her pants. She wanted Celia to know that she was wet already, and just the thought of her anticipated visit got her into such a state.

Wrapping her body behind Shannon, Celia started touching her extremely gently: caressing her hair, running a finger over her labia. Just enough of a tug that it didn't quite part. She gave her cunt a chance to wake up—but also ensuring Shannon was getting just a little less than what she wanted. When Shannon pushed Celia's hand firmly into her, she finally gave her more and increased the pace.

Celia turned Shannon so they faced each other, and placed her other hand over Shannon's neck—carefully, since she had said she liked things a little rough, but they hadn't talked about breath play. Shannon smiled, and released a quiet, "Yes." Without restricting or choking, Celia pushed her backwards. With her other hand pressed firmly into her clit and making small circles, Celia walked her backwards into the living room and got her onto the soft carpeted floor.

Shannon quickly kicked her pants half off and Celia laid down beside her. Celia's hand never left her cunt and she held Shannon tight. Celia moved a finger down to explore her opening, and Shannon instinctively thrust upward, matching Celia's rhythm. Starting with one finger, she moved to two, then three. Shannon snaked a hand up Celia's shirt and fondled her breast. Celia moved her thumb over Shannon's clit, sensing that she was close to coming. Celia freed one nipple from her bra and offered it to Shannon's mouth, then bore down and kept thrusting at a fast and consistent pace. She came, with muffled shouts yelled into Celia's chest.

Celia was still a bit nervous about sharing her whole body with Shannon. No matter how much someone says they are okay with the trans thing, you never know how they'll react when the pants come off. Will they be disgusted, or will they be way too into it?

So she took a baby step. Celia pulled a glove from her bag and asked Shannon to finger her, then started touching herself. Shannon needed some guidance and clearly hadn't done much anal play before, but once she started pressing in for that "come hither" motion, it rocketed Celia towards an explosive orgasm. She had to tell Shannon to stop when it got to be too much. At first Shannon thought Celia was stopping her because she had done something wrong. Then Celia explained she had come really hard, she just didn't squirt with every orgasm.

They cuddled, half-naked on the floor, for an hour or so. Sometimes chatting and getting to know someone works even better right after a good fuck. Celia thought Shannon was really starting to grow on her, even despite so much of her life that Shannon didn't understand. But the more they talked and the more Shannon asked about things it became clear she was genuinely interested and concerned.

Celia talked about the prejudice she faced. The insidious ways that prejudice manifested as discomfort, and that people would assume if she made them feel uncomfortable it must be because of something she did. It seemed like all it took was the slightest justification for everyone, from employers to cis queers to her family, to kick her to the curb. Celia mentioned running a GoFundMe fundraiser for her friend's recent medical costs. Everyone had pitched in a little, but when everyone you would turn to is facing the same material discrimination, it's that much harder to get what you need.

The conversation veered from poverty to classism to capitalism to sex work. Shannon didn't have much to add, but she followed along pretty well. She was shocked that she hadn't heard of FOSTA. Shannon knew who her representative was and immediately looked up to see if they had voted for it.

Overall, the connection was showing more promise. But the conversation was also a reminder of how different their worlds were. Celia wondered if a deeper connection would be possible with someone who was so completely unaware of things that were such a big deal in her world. But maybe that was something that could change.

The conversation began to lull, and they stared at each other for a while. Eventually Shannon broke the silence and said, "I think I'm really into you."

She gave Celia a passionate kiss. One thing led to another, and Celia was eating her out when her husband came home. She was so wrapped up in what she was doing that Celia didn't realize what was happening until Shannon tapped her on the head and called out to her husband, "Oh, honey! We lost track of time!"

Celia panicked for a moment as visions of a large angry man flashed through her head, but when she turned around there was a skinny guy awkwardly shuffling from side to side. Celia realized she could probably take him in a fight, and she found that surprisingly reassuring. He greeted her but clearly had no idea what to do in the situation.

"Well, uh, I guess I'll let you finish," he said, and he headed to the other room. On her way out he made a point of thanking Celia for visiting and wished her a good night. Celia laughed about it on the way home. All considering, it was pretty nice of him. To her surprise, when she got home she saw that Shannon had given a hundred dollars to the GoFundMe.

The next time they met, Shannon brought a bouquet of flowers. Celia placed them in a vase, appreciative but thinking it perhaps cost fifty dollars and she would much rather have the money.

Celia cooked dinner this time, a bubbling pot of lentils, potatoes, and apples that she hopes will feed her for the week.

They had a pattern at this point. After eating a light meal they headed to the bedroom. They were establishing an ease and comfort. One that was interrupted with the phrase, "I want you inside me."

Celia paused. That's not a kind of sex she usually did. It's not that she didn't do it, she just was unsure if that was something she was comfortable with at this point.

Shannon flushed and tried to explain that was not what she meant. "Just, like, your fingers, a toy, or whatever you want. I'm not expecting you to, um, I couldn't even do that with you."

"Why not?"

Shannon explained that she and her husband had only recently opened up their relationship. They had an agreement that Shannon can date other women but not men, and are particularly concerned about penetrative sex. "We jokingly call it the One Penis Policy."

Celia's blood went cold. If Shannon truly saw her as a woman, this wouldn't apply to her at all. "Penis" is not a word that she used for herself. Now she wondered if that was how Shannon saw that part of her body. Or even more concerning, how would her husband see things? She shared these concerns with Shannon, who was immediately apologetic.

Shannon tried to backpedal. Of course she was going to use whatever language Celia uses for herself. But that still left the question of whether or not that particular kind of sex was off limits. It sounded like it was. An agreement like that is set up because the husband sees the idea of his wife having sex with a man as more threatening than her having sex with a woman. If this policy applied to her, what did that say about who she was?

"I don't know if he'll think it applies to you," Shannon explained. "He doesn't even know that you're trans."

"You haven't told him that I'm trans?"

"It didn't seem like it was any of his business."

The whole argument killed the mood. They talked about it for another twenty minutes, and finally Celia just didn't want to deal with it anymore. She asked Shannon to leave. This was supposed to be easy. To just be for the sex. Now, with these hard feelings, thinking about the complicated and difficult discussions coming her way. Celia had to wonder if this was really what she wanted.

It was over a week until they saw each other again. That gave Celia a chance to stew in this new information. It made her resentful of him—of both of them. Because Shannon wasn't together enough to know if her husband was a transphobe, now Celia had to wait and see if this guy she met once is going to be bigoted enough to think of her as a man and shut down the whole thing.

The situation forced Celia to realize how disposable she was in this relationship. She felt like she was just waiting to be thrown away. The more she prepared herself for that reality, the more her feelings for Shannon began to go away. Everything was crumbling, all over a type of sex she didn't usually have. The more she thought about it, though, the more she wanted to do it just to spite them.

"It's my clit, by the way." Celia got right into it when they met up next time. "It's not a penis. I really don't like it being called that. I don't want you to think of my body that way. So if you're going to be talking about this with your husband, at least call it a clit."

Shannon had been worried that this would continue to be an issue. "I'm so sorry. It was a language slip. I never liked this plan, but I just want to hook up with women so I agreed to it to make him feel better about the whole open marriage thing," Shannon explained. "But you're right. I don't even have to talk with him about it. You're a woman. You don't have a penis. This doesn't apply to us."

Hearing that made Celia feel better. They moved on to other conversation. Shannon gave her another fifty-dollar bouquet of flowers. Celia vaguely wondered how much money her husband had. But it was all too late to undo the damage. Celia didn't think about the relationship in the same way anymore. She had reminded herself so many times that this was just about sex that she was letting go of any attachment she had.

Shannon kissed her, and Celia softened—just a little. They moved to the bedroom and Celia threw Shannon down to the bed. She gasped and smiled, then pulled Celia down on top of her. Celia realized she was being a bit more aggressive than usual. It seemed to be working well.

"So, really, that policy doesn't apply to us?" Celia asked.

"Yeah, I feel good about this decision. I'm following his request to just date women. There's no penis here, just clits. He doesn't need to know anything more about who I'm involved with."

"So we can do whatever we want with my clit?" Celia raised an eyebrow, suggestively.

"Oh! You're okay with that?" There was a lot Shannon still didn't know about how Celia liked to have sex, and had prepared herself for that kind of penetration being off limits. Now that she was considering it a possibility, she was very enthusiastic. "I'd really like that."

Celia was already hard and took a moment to grab a condom. She held Shannon down by the shoulder with one hand while playing with her clit with the other. Shannon grabbed her hips and pulled. They both moaned when Celia entered her.

Celia slowly built up speed. The undercurrent of frustration and anger spurred her on. Shannon was giving back just as much. She pulled away and turned around. "Fuck me from behind."

Shannon was on her hands and knees, one hand on her clit. Her ass rippled with each impact and she felt the force travel through her body. "Yes, keep going!"

Celia was having a hard time focusing on what it felt like. She moved mechanically. She noticed Shannon was getting close, so she sped up even more. She was working with all that her muscles could give when Shannon came. Then suddenly she realized that she was coming, too.

As they lay together on the bed, Celia tried to examine what she was feeling. Shannon smiled at her. This was a good fuck after an argument, a time to make up and reconnect. She could feel how much Shannon wanted that. But then what? Celia couldn't risk opening up, again. Not when she was acutely aware of how easy it would be for her to be discarded.

Later that evening, Celia was working on a message to Shannon's husband. She wasn't going to wait until he eventually found out. She was going to out herself, and tell him what they did. A part of her hoped that he just didn't care. That he was all enlightened and trans supportive. But if that was the case, how likely would he have been to set up a rule like the One Penis Policy? More likely, he was insecure. He needed to be in control. He needed women to be uncomplicated, not capable of deep relationships, and cis.

Sending this letter without checking in first would probably mean that things with Shannon would be over, and Celia accepted that. It would cause problems with her husband. He might think Shannon lied to him. He might think she cheated on their agreement. He might be furious. He might want a divorce.

The more Celia thought about it, though, she realized that she hoped that is exactly what he would do. She hit send and went to bed.

THE SUMMER OF STRAP-ONS AND SODOMY

Rain DeGrey

We first met over a mutual love of both strap-on sex and getting paid for it. Getting paid to do what you love feels like winning the lottery. It tastes delicious. To meet someone in the course of doing what you love and fall for them hard? It doesn't get much better than that.

"There is someone I want you to meet," one of my favorite clients said to me after a vigorous session. We were laying in a blissful puddle of spent endorphins and he was staring up at the ceiling with a purposeful look on his face. "Her name is Kara. You would love her. I know you two would definitely get along."

"Sure thing," I replied. "Happy to do so." I've always been open-minded and was curious who would inspire him to make such a strong statement. What was the worst that could happen? He was wrong? What if he was right? A small hopeful animal poked its head out in the landscape of my mind. I was single and over it. Pro domme work only checked so many boxes. There was space in my life for something new and exciting. Maybe that thing was named Kara.

Arrangements were made and the three of us set up to meet for a co-topping strap-on session about a week later. I've always enjoyed co-topping sessions—the energy and flow can be such a rewarding headspace if done properly. There is a fluid unspoken language if the right groove is hit, the language of flesh and desire and power.

The week passed quickly, but not quickly enough. I had to admit, I was counting down the days. At the appointed time, I waited for them outside the building where I rented out a room for session work, running my fingers over its rough stone exterior. It was still radiating from the stored heat of the day. I amused myself by thinking about all of the illicit orgasms that had occurred within the unassuming walls. The residents living there had no idea. The thought gave me a secret thrill. For me, the forbidden has always been more appealing.

Eager to begin, I kept one eye on the clock. My head buzzed with anticipation. The summer evening was warm and that familiar thrill of sex and money was in my blood. The night held an edgy promise of something interesting in the wind. Then my client Carl turned the corner with Kara in tow—and that potential promise of interesting crystallized into reality.

I could instantly tell that she was a powerful package of sexuality contained by a tiny five-foot-two frame. Her body was exceptionally toned, years of classical ballet training had shaped it into a lean weapon. Her waist was so small I could almost encircle it with my big hands.

Kara had almost no breasts to speak of, any natural tendency towards them combated by extensive exercise. Long straight black hair flowed down to her waist and her brown eyes looked slightly mischievous and up to no good. All this was accentuated by her dance-trained butt which jutted out enthusiastically. I craved to use it as a pillow on which to rest my head at night. Someone that lean had no right to have that glorious of a butt. Not that I was complaining.

Was she my type? Yes. Yes she was. And then some.

I wanted to throw her over my shoulder like a Maine Coon cat and have intellectual conversations with her in between bouts of sodomy.

Towering over her, I thrust out my hand, trying to play it cool. "Hey there Kara. Rain. Pleasure to meet you."

She looked up at me with those mischievous brown eyes and I knew I was in trouble. "Kara," she said, sliding her small hand into mine and pumping it up and down confidently. "Likewise."

The strap-on session was a blur of sex and exhilaration. We hit it off so well that we basically ignored the man that brought us together. Carl was the meat in a sandwich of paid-for bread slices that were so busy being dazzled with each other that the meat went unloved. As we Eiffel Towered him on both ends, we made flirty faces across his bent-over body. He was distracted and didn't notice our building sexual tension, or if he did, perhaps he thought he was the source. By the end of the session, Kara and I had exchanged phone numbers and made plans for a date.

Normally, first dates involve some trepidation and nerves. Not this one. It was effortless, as if we had known each other for years. There was no nervousness, just the thrill of meeting someone who was obviously one of my people—someone cut from the same cloth. We tumbled headlong into a relationship. It was as natural and effortless as breathing.

Our days together were long and languid. We were well-paid sex workers, with a belief in endless time that accompanies the inexperience of youth. There wasn't anything we couldn't do and the air around us was a heady incense of weed and relaxation as we passed our time sunbathing in Golden Gate Park—our blanket a life raft against the cares of the world. When I cuddled up against her, the rest of the world dropped away. More than anything, I felt comfortable around her. She was a judgment-free zone.

During these times, lounging like two cats in the sun, I got to know her better. She told me how she used to cut class in high school to meet up with a rich businessman for strap-on pro domme sessions, a revolt against her conservative upbringing. Her parents' arranged marriage was a failure and they got on with the business of raising their children and staying out of each other's hair.

Her mother had long ago realized that she was a lesbian and moved into the living room. It wasn't talked about, like many things in her family. Kara would complain to me how awkward it was for her to go to the Lex and see her mother on the other end of the bar as they studiously avoided making eye contact with each other. Luckily they didn't have the same taste in women or it could've easily turned into a Jerry Springer episode with a San Francisco twist.

Our nights together were often spent with me watching her dance at Divas. Her fluid sexuality, like mine, would bleed over the edges and make messy watercolors. Everything about her was fascinating to me and somehow, unbelievably, she was mine.

After an evening of building up sexual tension, watching her gyrate against hungry customers as they stuffed wads of cash into her lingerie—the hope of sharing just a few brief moments of fantasy with her—I would take her home and assfuck her in her tiny bedroom, a closet under the stairs of her parents' house.

I would hold her compact body face down and ass up, my clit fully engorged against the base of my strap-on, and feel the ripples of bliss move through me as I entered her from behind. Pressing her head deeply into the pillows with one hand, the other holding her back down, listening to the squeals of pleasure bubbling up as we rode that wave. It was an endless marvel to me, her raw and honest appetite. No matter what I dished out, she took and asked for more.

That perfect ass was like a magnet to me, I simply could not get enough of it. Kara would have to bite down on the pillows so her moans would not drift up through the old wooden floorboards and disturb her parents. She was a splayed out butterfly, pinned down as she writhed in her bedsheets, her long black hair trailing across the pillows. She was all ass and hair and endless desire. Lucky, lucky me. Her flesh felt like a perfect fit against mine.

I don't think her parents ever even knew I was there. Or if they did, they decided not to say anything. We kept our voices pitched low and I never ventured into any other parts of the house. It was a matter of respect—and explaining the sex worker under the stairs would have been an awkward conversation to have. The fact that I was a woman would only have made it worse. It was a house of secrets and suppressed sexuality.

The highlight of our magical summer together was organizing a strap-on gangbang session with our respective clients. Kara was the one that came up with it, bless her entrepreneurial little heart.

"I know a place in the Mission we could rent out!" she told me. "We should get our regulars together and have a strap-on orgy! Wouldn't that be hot? You and me working them all over and them paying us for the privilege?"

I had to admit she made a convincing pitch. You only live once and strap-on orgy with my girlfriend would be a cool thing to check off my bucket list. Not that I had even been aware it was on my bucket list until she had proposed it.

"Let's do it," I told her. Because why the heck not? The fact that it was complex and not exactly legal only added to the appeal to me.

We pitched the concept to our regulars and once we got enough interested people signed up, put together a truly epic strap-on orgy. Towels were purchased. Lube was stocked. Condoms were stockpiled. Toys were assembled. I was *ready*.

The night of the orgy got off to a slow start, as orgies occasionally do, but before long things picked up momentum and the train left the station. As everyone loosened up and relaxed, the room became a blur of bent-over bodies cradled in towel-draped pillows while Kara and I prowled about and dished out pleasure, never losing eye contact with each other. Our clients on the other had avoided it, guiltily turned on by the whole thing but unable to truly appreciate the moment. Not Kara and I. We were empowered and vibrating, sexual goddess reveling in our connection.

After thoroughly pegging every available butt, it was our turn for a grand finale. Time to show them what people without hangups could do. It is amazing the freedom that not giving a fuck gives you.

Taking out some rope from my handy bag of tricks, I tied Kara down spread-eagle on the floor. There were no secure tie points in the room, so I improvised it using the furniture in the room. Weaving around couch and table legs, I bound her down as she looked up at me with eager anticipatory eyes. It was messy, but it would get the job done. She looked like a spider in the middle of a large hemp web.

Using my trusty Hitachi and an extension cord, I crouched down and began lightly teasing that tight, flushed slit that was already slick with her juices. There was no rush. We had time. Heat rose off her flesh in fragrant waves. Kara strained and wiggled, moaning through gritted teeth, sliding into the undone places as she chanted my name under her breath, cursing and thanking me simultaneously.

I pulled out orgasm after orgasm from her bound body. Like me, Kara ran highly multi-orgasmic. I gleefully used that fact against her. Involuntary shudders ran through her flesh as waves of pleasure crashed over her. The more she pulled on the ropes, the stronger her orgasms were. Her face was slack and glassy-eyed with bliss, her pink tongue licked her lips, a greedy kitten with a bowl of milk.

The room smelled of sex and bodies. All of that teasing was only a warm up—just revving the engine of her pussy. I was setting the foundation for what was yet to come. Once Kara was off leash, I knew she was going to transform from greedy kitten into a fierce cheetah. A cheetah I couldn't wait to face.

Eagerly I untied her from the various pieces of furniture, setting the cheetah free. Grabbing my Hitachi out of my hand, she shoved me to the ground in a swift confident moment. She was dance-trained fluid and stronger than she looked. I didn't object. The view from where I was sitting was quite nice indeed. Putting one dainty and perfectly pedicured foot up on my chest between my breasts, Kara stood over me, swaying slightly. "Get on your back," she whispered, her eyes shining.

"Gladly," I whispered back, looking up at the fascinating folds and subtle shades of her labia, swollen and full from orgasms and vibrator use. Slick juices ran out of her pussy and down her thighs. I wanted to swim in them. It was as if the secrets of the universe were contained in there and all I had to do was find them out. I lay down flat to receive my fate. My toes wiggled in hungry anticipation.

Wielding the Hitachi in one expert hand while straddling me, Kara worked her way up to an explosive squirting orgasm and then unleashed all over me. It was like being drenched with a firehose. How she could contain so much come in such a tiny body is one of the great mysteries that shall never be solved. There was so much that it ran across my face, pooling into my ears and collecting in warm little puddles. The room suddenly shifted to underwater squishy sounds, I was having a hard time hearing. Vaguely, I could make out the low rumble of people talking around me but everything was muffled. I was literally deafened by her come. The taste of her was in my mouth and running into my hair.

Fumbling around half-blind, I latched onto a nearby hand towel. Tilting my head, I drained out onto it as Kara stood over me triumphant and amused, waving the Hitachi around the awed room like a scepter. Her perky nipples pierced the air and her chest heaved from the exertion. The assembled crowd looked as impressed as I felt. We were all glowing. Strap-on orgy success.

Driving home that night, I was so high on dopamine and oxytocin, it was as if my bones were lighter. Clutching the steering wheel and tapping along to the beat blasting from the speakers, I kept catching glimpses of my grinning and flushed face in the rearview mirror. I looked as if I had won the lottery. And had I not? A hot ballerina with a high sex drive who was down with being my partner in nefarious activity and accepted me as I was? It doesn't get much better than that.

I sang along badly to the radio, come still in my ear. The bits of squirt I had missed with the towel felt like tight hugs on my skin as they dried, little bits of her left behind for me to remember her by. Cars passing by had no idea, and a pleased and satisfied smile beamed from my face. How many of them were heading home from a successful orgy their girlfriend had organized, still covered in her come? Not many, if I were to guess.

The end of our glorious summer was inevitable—everything shifts and the only constant is change. I still think about her, now and then, when the warm wind shifts and there is a smell of marijuana in the air. Suddenly we will be back on our blanket in Golden Gate Park, young and content and snuggled up next to each other without a care in the world. I hope wherever she is now, she is happy. I wonder if she still thinks about me. I will never know, but we will always have our summer of strap-ons and sodomy. I will always carry a piece of her in my heart, a feisty fearless ballerina that did exactly what she wanted. Nobody has ever come in my ear since.

STRAND OF PEARLS

Mary P. Burns

I'm sitting in an intimate bar on 1st Avenue near 74th Street, one table away from a crackling fire and one frosted French window away from the bitter cold of a January night. The perfect distance for warmth and reminiscence. A Japanese single malt whisky occupies the coaster in front of me. They've become very adept, the Japanese, at making the smoky, silky, amber liquid that goes down like honey and then kicks you back, leaving an afterburn in your throat that tastes of charred logs on a brazier. She always comes to mind in moments like this. Sultry. Smoky. Silky. Skin so smooth. Everywhere. A voice like honey . . . and her scent, like burning maple leaves in the fall. Bonfire, her perfume was called. "The bottled essence of autumn on fire in the Northeast," she'd said. And it was.

I still can't walk anywhere in September or October that her presence isn't all around me in the woodsy effluence of the earth shutting down for the winter. Nor can I walk past some restaurants where we went to lunch, stores we lingered in looking at things, innocently touching each other as we talked instead of admitting we wanted to take each other to bed.

I can see us in her bed, though, finally, that soft skin under my palms, my hands overflowing with her generous breasts as she lay back against me, her hard nipples between my gently squeezing fingers, my nose buried in her hair the color of winter wheat—gold with caramel tones. It smells of almonds.

My cock would lie useless in my pants on those afternoons, the pants themselves somewhere on the floor strewn among the rest of our things. She didn't want it. Not the first time I made love to her nor the last. "But you're married," I had said. I would later learn she kept these precious hours from her husband out of respect for him, as he did with his paramours for her.

She understood the implication and looked at me with just a hint of pity in her smile. I was confused. It was my largest cock, with a lovely girth to it. Most women were nearly overcome when they saw it, having sought me out because I'd garnered a bit of a reputation as a skilled, artful lover after my friend Dominick had taught me how to roll my hips and thrust just so one humid August afternoon when I'd confessed to him that I'd bought the apparatus but wasn't a hundred percent sure how to best use it. We'd gone through six watermelons in those three hours.

"You're sweet to take that into consideration," she'd said that first afternoon, caressing my cheek. We'd only gotten as far as kissing, carefully removing each other's clothes before tossing our shirts, her skirt, bra, and panties, on the floor, she'd dropped my trousers and disengaged my harness, letting it fall, too. "We have an open marriage. I like his cock very much." She'd taken my hands, kissed each fingertip, brushed her nose against the nipples of my small breasts, like Eskimo kisses. "You have something else I want." She'd slid her finger into my mouth, found my tongue.

I understood the implication.

She didn't mention the razor at first.

We'd met the previous winter when I landed a coveted in-house temp position at one of the major ad agencies in the city. This meant I'd be under contract the entire three years that I'd also be in graduate school. The agency willing to work with my class schedule. It was a gig I desperately needed, so I could support myself while I got my MBA. Since I hardly looked the part, though, I wasn't sure I'd get the job. In those days, they wanted corporate polish. I was tall and gangly, and wore a modified Marine buzz cut and three-piece suits from Joseph A. Bank that I could only afford when they had sales. And wing tips, of course. But all Kathy Williams in HR saw when she interviewed me was a hundred and twenty words per minute, dictation, the dying art of shorthand, French, Spanish, and "not opposed to running personal errands."

I'd been there just nine months when Kathy needed a top-notch assistant for the executive floor and found she didn't have anyone on the current staff to turn to except for me. I was aware those assignments went to the straight girls who looked like secretarial extras on *Mad Men*, who "fit in." I'd also heard all about the perks of working the executive floor from the girls who'd been—the free lunches, afternoon tea cart, company cars home if overtime was worked—but through attrition and vacations, there was no other temp left with my skill set, so Kathy had no choice. She didn't ask me to change my appearance. She simply told me to quietly go above and beyond, let my natural abilities shine, and find a way to bond with both the executives and their assistants, become part of the team, because I'd be there for three months working for the one female executive on that floor. I knew from office gossip that Pamela had been the CEO's secretary and long-time mistress for years before he gave her a corner office and the title "Special Assistant" that meant nothing but that she'd molded into meaning everything in that arena, becoming the de facto lion tamer and wielding a sharp whip at board meetings and private meetings alike. None of that kind of politics mattered to me, though. I was enough of an anomaly that no one ever knew what to do with me or how to treat me, so power games just washed off me, leaving me free to do my job.

When the elevator doors opened that morning, the heady atmosphere hit me first: the elegant men's club décor of oak and walnut, thick rugs, wingback chairs. While portraits of past CEOs graced the walls, the hushed semblance of weighty decisions hung in the air, mingled with the trace of cigar smoke.

The fire crackles and pops, I take a sip of my whisky and consider the flames jumping in the fireplace. Millenials with their open-floor grass-roots start-ups have made such halls of power a cliché everywhere except on Wall Street. But that winter, they were very much alive.

The pretty young receptionist phoned Pamela to let her know I was there, and sent me back to her office. I heard her on the phone, put my messenger bag down on the assistant's desk, aware that no one was looking at me but all eyes were on me, and took the small spiral notebook from it that I used in those temp jobs. I stepped close enough to the door to see inside her office without her seeing me, waiting for the call to end so I could introduce myself. This room exuded a different kind of authority than the rest of the floor, a study in French blue and cream, Duncan Phyfe furniture, vases of pink roses on several surfaces. The Cassatt on the wall was real; there was a tiny red wire peeking out from behind the lower right corner of it.

When she hung up, I knocked and walked in. She stood, came out from behind her desk, hand extended. Her regal beauty stole the breath I would've used to say my name. My eyes took in every inch of her without ever leaving her face until her hand was in mine and I looked down at the long delicate fingers, the perfectly manicured nails, and blushed. The navy stilettos matched her suit. Her toned figure statuesque, she was as tall as me, and when I looked back into those blue-and-diamond eyes, I saw a gorgeous woman of a certain age in that last blaze of mature beauty before time would rob her of everything, leaving her invisible to the world. And I fell in love. A strand of pearls rested between the hollow of her neck and her cleavage, and I desperately wanted to kiss each bead. Instead, I took the index card from her as she spoke and perused the list of names on both sides, people she needed to talk with today on one side, people she'd be "unavailable at the moment" for on the other side.

"You've come prepared," she said, nodding at the notebook. "I like that." Her eyes moved all the way down to my wingtips and back up to my dark brown eyes, and stayed there. Another woman had once told me that the flecks of gold that speckled my irises made them look like galaxies in the night sky. I wondered if she was seeing that. "You can take a letter." She sat back down at her desk and we got to work as though we'd been doing this together for years.

Back at my desk, I looked over the instruction manual her assistant had left me, found her computer ID and password, and set to transcribing Pamela's letter for a Mail Merge. A moment later, the chief legal officer's assistant was in front of my desk introducing herself, asking if I needed anything, and inviting me to lunch. With Kathy's advice to become part of the team whispering in my ear, I said "Yes." As the week passed, the seven other assistants on the floor came by to introduce themselves, ask if I needed anything, and invite me to lunch. It felt a bit like a secret society at work, but it was also a bird's eye view into how the floor functioned, each woman imparting information to me at lunch that fit neatly into a puzzle that helped me negotiate the politics, the other executives, and Pamela, whom they all knew well.

Each morning I was at my desk at eight thirty, shortly before Pamela arrived, ready to serve her every need, staying until she was finished for the day. More than once she told me to go home at five, but I couldn't. Something in me needed to be near her.

The holiday season proved hectic; I ran many errands for her, most of them related to corporate business, but one or two personal, all of them in a company car. I got back very late one evening after going to a Connecticut saddlery to pick up a saddle she'd had handmade for her husband, a champion rider. I'd waited almost two hours for the artisan's finishing touches, putting my return at ten o'clock, but I brought the saddle right up to her office. And found her reclining on the sofa in the gown she'd worn to a fundraiser that evening.

"What happened?" she asked when I walked in, surprising her.

I stammered through my explanation, trying to keep my eyes on hers and not on the red silk of the gown swirling over her legs, hugging her waist and clinging to her breasts. The ever-present strand of pearls snuggled in her cleavage.

"You should've called me. You could've come back and gone out tomorrow." She sighed and rubbed her brows. "Some of these dog-and-pony shows are so exhausting."

I put the saddle down by the door and slid onto the couch, lifting her feet to my lap. She looked at me, dumbfounded, as I slipped her heels off and began massaging her left foot. She groaned, and her head fell back exposing that beautiful column of her neck. I wanted to crawl up the length of her and lick that neck right up to her mouth, kiss her hard, and then kiss back down to those breasts wrapped in red. She pulled the hem of her evening gown up to get it out of the way. Looking at me, she said, "Shorthand, dictation, and massage . . . you are a woman of many talents."

I hadn't taken my eyes from the hem as it moved, and now I stared at the curve of her calves; she raised the gown higher, inching it above her knees. My eyes met hers. I wasn't sure what to think. She raised it mid-thigh, and I thought I saw white pearls glistening in the darkness between her legs. "That's better," she said. I took her right foot in my hands. This time she moaned.

After a few minutes of working on both feet, I moved my hands up her left calf, and one of them to the front of her thigh, bracing her leg so I could knead the calf muscle. She raised a perfectly arched eyebrow. "It helps to loosen the ankle and calf muscles, too," I said as I worked on them, "keep everything in balance, but this is as far as I'm going."

"Yes, it is." The blue-and-diamond eyes had become hard even though I felt her trembling under my touch.

She let me work a little longer and then announced that she had to use the ladies' room, and then we'd both better go home. I accompanied her, having need of it myself, and took my time washing my hands when I was through so I could walk her down to her car. Suddenly I heard pinging and clattering and turned to see pearls bouncing everywhere. I began to gather them up. They were slick and I picked up the scent of musk from them, odd when I knew her perfume had a woodsy aroma to it. The door of her stall slammed open.

"I'll get those," she said.

I looked up at her from my place on the floor on my knees, my hand full of pearls, and saw that her necklace was intact. Glancing back at the pearls in my hand, I knew from whence they had come.

"There should be sixty of them," she said, a blush rising from her neck and reddening her cheeks. She held out her hands and I began to count pearls into them. Fifty-eight.

"That's fine," she said, flustered.

I stood up. "I'll find the other two tomorrow morning, before everyone gets here."

"No . . ."

I put my hand on her bare shoulder. Then, I opened one of the hand towels on the sink so she could put the pearls down, and I wrapped it tightly around them. Back at my desk, I taped the towel shut, helped her into her fur, and tucked the small package into the inside pocket of the coat. She looked at me, the blue-and-diamond eyes warm, and ran her fingers through my hair, which had gotten longer in the few weeks that I hadn't had time to attend to it.

"I've wondered since meeting you how that would feel . . ."

"I need to get it cut," I murmured.

"Don't," she said quickly. "Let it get a little longer."

I found the two errant pearls in the morning and left them in the cut glass ashtray that she kept on her desk for the CEO's cigar. I knew she'd see them there.

A few days later, Pamela took me to lunch. She'd just found out her assistant had decided not to return after maternity leave. "Would you stay with me?" she asked. "I know you're in school. We can keep the arrangement exactly as it is, except I've asked HR for a better salary."

"May I think about it?"

"Of course," she replied.

On the way back to the office, we stopped in a chocolate shop so she could get Christmas gifts for the assistants. As the counter girl wrapped the packages, she turned to me and straightened my tie. "Don't think too long. I really want you."

Throughout that winter and spring, she took me to lunch once a week to thank me, she said, for all my hard work. We roamed further and further from the neighborhood of the office in search of ever newer places, stopping in a store or boutique on the way back to look at things, finding ways to touch each other, a hand, a wrist, the small of a back, as we showed each other scarves or ties or pieces of jewelry we admired. One day we passed a specialty shaving shop, and she turned right around, went in, asked to see the razor that would give the closest shave. The gentleman behind the counter brought out two different electric shavers.

"No. For women."

He unlocked a case beneath the counter and set a tray of small electric razors in front of her. I watched Pamela study them, pick one up, run her thumb over the blades.

"And if I'm looking for non-electric?"

He took a tray from the same case. I wandered around the store as she looked at those. As much as I loved watching her hands touch anything, I was intrigued with this shop and wanted to know what else it carried. I spotted a small can of shaving cream called Captain's Choice 45th Parallel, a cherry/almond blend, opened it to sniff, and brought it up to the counter. Pamela picked it up and examined it, looked at me.

"I love that smell," I said. "It's like cherry pie."

She added it to her growing purchases.

"Oh, no, I can buy my own."

"Then go get another. For me."

Without thinking of the implications, I did.

One Friday afternoon in June, the inevitable happened, and I realized I'd been praying for it for weeks. We were the only two left on the floor at two o'clock on the first summer Friday, many of the executives not even having come in that day. Pamela was reaching for the plant on the top of the secretary as I put her files away in her desk. Seeing that even in her heels she'd be an inch short of it, I reached for the small stepping stool she sometimes used, put it in front of her, my hand on her waist, and she stumbled. I caught her. Surprised, she apologized, and then my mouth was on hers, her hand in the curls at the top of my head, her other hand on the back of my neck. Her lips were soft, but we were crushing each other, I could feel her teeth grinding into them, into mine. I moved my hands to cup her ass cheeks, pull them apart under her skirt, pull her skirt up so I could touch her lace panties. Then my hands were under them, on her bare bottom, and one of her hands went between my legs and I twitched. And she abruptly broke the kiss.

"What?" I asked. Had I done something wrong?

Then I felt her hand close around my cock. It was the largest one in my collection. I'd been wearing it for over a week, hoping I would need it soon.

"I thought you were a woman," she said.

"I am."

She let go of my cock.

"It's a harness. And a dildo."

"Why?"

"Because I like it."

She looked down at my crotch. When the blue-and-diamond eyes focused on me again, they were ablaze. She picked up her purse, took my hand, and walked to my desk. "Get your bag."

I stuffed my notebook into it thinking she was marching me down to HR to fire me. But once in the elevator, she pushed "G." We walked out the front doors of the building, headed south and after three blocks, turned onto a side street. She walked up the front steps of a five-story brownstone and unlocked the front door. Inside, it was clear to see that this was a private home. Without a word, she led me past an elegantly appointed living room to an elevator beneath the wide walnut stairs that spiraled up to the second floor, pushed the fifth-floor button, and we rode up in silence. She took my hand when the elevator stopped and the door opened, and pulled me down a carpeted hallway to a large bedroom. Sun suffusing through the gauzy white curtains gave the room a hazy feel. Pamela dropped my hand and took off her heels as I looked around the room, the walls antique white, the carpeting underfoot a sea blue, couches and chairs matching it, a writing desk angled to look out the window piled with papers, and then Pamela was unbuttoning my shirt, slowly, almost gingerly, and I forgot what was in the room or underfoot as I began undressing her. Every few buttons, we kissed, slow, lingering, coming together like we were underwater, and then moving to another piece of clothing until we stood naked in front of each other and she was kissing my fingers, putting one of hers in my mouth and telling me she wanted me for something other than the cock that lay on the floor in my pants. I went to remove her strand of pearls and she stopped me. She liked to wear them when anyone made love to her. My clitoris hardened.

She walked me into the bathroom where one of the razors she'd bought at the specialty shop sat daintily on a towel next to a small shave brush. Next to them was the Captain's Choice 45th and a bowl. I looked at her blankly.

"I want you to shave me first."

"Shave you?" I was confused for the second time in just minutes.

She took my hand and put it between her legs. I felt the soft hair there. And it dawned on me. I got very nervous.

"But . . ."

She put her finger on my lips. "I'll walk you through it. We'll talk as you work."

"I'll cut you. By accident!" I blurted.

"You won't. I promise. I also promise you'll give me a powerful orgasm this way."

That shut me up. I had never considered that.

"I'll teach you. And along the way, you'll learn that this intimate act is so much more than that . . ." She pointed in the direction of my cock. Then she kissed me, her tongue finding mine as she rubbed her hands ever so slightly over my nipples, sending shivers up my spine. I pulled her closer, wanting those ample breasts and hard nipples on my own, quivering at the sensation of my clit throbbing, getting hard in anticipation of my tongue on her button, but she gently pulled away.

"No. Not yet." She handed me the razor and brush, leaned in to whisper in my ear. "I'm a mess, wanting you. Please . . . make me come." She picked up a towel from the corner of the claw-footed tub. "Fill that bowl with warm water and bring it to the bed."

She was stretched out on the bed like a Dionysian nymph, a small round stool by the bottom of it. At her feet were a dainty silver butt plug and a short, thick dildo. "Would you do something for me?" she asked, her voice an octave lower, thick with need as I stood holding the bowl.

Anything . . .

"Would you choose one of those for your ass before you sit down?"

I put the bowl down on the table she'd left by the chair, picked up the butt plug, and immersed it in the warm water. Then, her eyes hungrily devouring my every move, I bent, put my hand between my legs, and guided it into my anus. A sigh escaped her, and she smiled. Then I picked up the dildo, put it in my mouth, and Pamela gasped as I wet it thoroughly. Because I was certain it would drive her crazy, I straddled the stool, looked down at my pussy, put my hand at the top of it to pull myself open, looked directly at her, and slid the thick toy inside. Those blue-and-diamond eyes went wide, sparkled with fear and excitement; I lowered myself onto the stool, took hold of her ankles, and pulled her toward me, moving around carefully on the stool until I found a comfortable angle to sit, her pussy inches from my nose.

She was breathing heavily as I opened the jar of shaving cream, but I put it down, pushed her bent knees to the bed, leaned in, and swiped my tongue through her pussy, kissed her clitoris as a strangled noise emerged from her throat.

"I shouldn't be aroused as you shave me," she whispered. "Please don't . . ."

I swallowed hard, my own clit now pounding, and dipped the brush into the jar. "What do I do?"

"Cover me in the cream, everywhere there's hair," she answered breathlessly.

I did so slowly, thoroughly, as she moaned quietly.

"Now, carefully start up here," she indicated the slight paunch of her stomach down to her mons Venus. "All the way across, working your way down to my . . ." She groaned as I caressed her inner thighs, picked up the razor, and began carefully shaving. I worked quickly, efficiently, impatient to get to those lips that had been shielded by a fine blonde down, a smattering of gray coming in. Having rinsed the razor so many times, I had to change the water in the bowl. My walk to the bathroom brought admiring remarks from Pamela.

Upon my return, her bent knees were flat on the bed for the delicate operation of shaving her tender labia. I wiped her clean, then I moved to the side of the bed, leaned over, kissed her breasts, and took each nipple into my mouth as she ran her hands over my back, put one hand between my legs, and pushed at the stubby dildo, which almost popped out, and I nearly came. She banished me to my stool although I wanted so much more of her breasts. I ground my ass on it to push both tools in, and to scratch the itch of my pounding clit as I lathered her pussy with cream.

Then, as she directed me, I moved the razor through the groin muscles, parted her lips, and maneuvered it through row after tiny row of the cherry-scented icing. She wriggled between each swath, I drew my finger up the center of her sex to keep my path clear and she'd moan, rock a little, and I'd respond with rocking of my own to tamp down the pounding between my lips.

I'd "accidentally" touch her clitoris and she'd protest; I'd put the tip of my thumb into her anus and she rewarded me with a gravelly groan; then I'd have to touch myself, the excitement growing between both of us until finally, all that was left was a little landing strip. I wiped the remainder of the cream from her and touched the tip of my tongue to her clitoris. She shuddered and I drove my tongue straight into her, plunging in and out of her as she shook uncontrollably, her newly shaved pussy an exposed land that I conquered.

She tried to shut her legs, I climbed up onto the bed to lick and suck her nipples, two of my fingers inside her, and I made her come again. As the tremors slowly subsided, I kissed her, drinking her in, gathered her to me, pulled back the covers, and settled us in a block of diffused sun.

She lay back against me, my hands full with her breasts, playing with her nipples, and we talked. She wanted to know about what I wanted from life. I wanted to know about her husband, but before I could ask, she sat up and removed the stubby dildo from me and went down on me, gently twisting the butt plug as she expertly worked her tongue, eliciting the most astounding orgasm I'd ever had. Then she held me in her arms, the afternoon sun slanting across the bed.

I left before her husband came home. It was a ritual we would repeat weekly for two more years, until my contract was up. I had my degree in my hand, and she had opened doors that helped me land a job at a new tech company that would eventually grow into a behemoth, and as I rose through the ranks, with her guidance during weekly phone calls, I eventually moved onto the executive floor first as an EVP and then becoming the CEO.

I still use Captain's Choice 45th, though. And, sometimes, I keep a strand of pearls in my pocket.

RESTRAINT

Kiki DeLovely

I take my time preparing your coffee. Meticulously measuring exactly 100 ml, adding a healthy splash of half-and-half, pouring the coconut water over that one large, solitary ice cube until I've got the proportions just right. Or at least I *hope* I do. My heartbeat quickens a bit as I begin my ascent upstairs with my offering in hand, praying that it will please you.

My heartbeat jumps into my clit the moment I lay eyes on you—relaxing there on the sofa with an air of self-confidence, looking so fucking handsome, my knees just about give out. And so I give into that inclination, dropping to my knees in front of you. You take the offering from my outstretched hands, an approving smile gracing your face.

I don't move. Don't even breathe as I watch you bring the cup to your lips. Anxiously awaiting the completion of that first sip, my eyes drop down to your throat as I observe your swallow.

"*Mmmm* . . . that's perfect."

Only then do I realize I was holding my breath. I exhale audibly, relieved and reveling in your praise, beaming up at you.

You rub your free hand along my face and then comb through my hair with your strong fingers. I melt into your touch, basking in the physical reassurance you're so generous with. Your hands always make me feel so safe, provide a level of comfort and security when words are lacking. You pull my head into your lap, sweetly, tenderly. Delighting in the textured feel of your jeans against my cheek, I nuzzle against you as you continue stroking my hair, enjoying your coffee, your view. Your eyes poring over the details of my vintage slip—trailing along the light blue ruffled trim, you take in how the fabric is the palest shade of lavender you've ever seen—barely a shade beyond white. A small part of you wants to tear it off me but you breathe into your composure instead, working your fingers more firmly against my scalp.

Maybe a little sigh escapes my lips. Maybe the softest moan.

"What a good girl. You did so well with my coffee this morning. I think you deserve a sip."

I eagerly accept your praise as you bring the cup to my lips. I do not touch the cup, my hands remain neatly folded in my lap—you control the precise amount of creamy brew you deem appropriate as a reward and I willingly welcome its entry. Smooth and barely bitter, mixed with just a hint of sweetness. It is perfection in my mouth. "*Mmmmmmmmm* . . . Thank you, Sir."

I gaze up at you as you survey me from above, no words necessary in a moment like this. You admiring that look in my eyes, me drowning in that look in yours. Plummeting into subspace. The tension tightening between us. But still you take your time.

For once, I'm not in a hurry either. Content to curl up at your feet, reveling in my place of honor, my body in no rush to go anywhere. I could stay here all day.

That is, until you run the flat of your hand up the back of my neck, snaking across the base of my skull, and gradually start to *squeeeeeze*. Curling your fingers tautly, helping yourself to a generous fistful of my hair, you slowly pull my head back down into your lap. I relish the warmth and rigidity in your thighs against my cheekbone, sense the heat surging from your crotch. I inhale you deeply, smelling your desire that rises up to meet mine. Sharp, carnal notes penetrating my nostrils. I gasp as you get a little rougher, shoving me against you just a little, my cunt clenching up. These actions of yours make me hungry, greedy, make me need so much more.

You know this. Keenly aware of what you're doing, leaning into your sadistic side ever so slightly. You long to feel the softness of my sweet tongue against you, to watch my crimsoned lips wrapped around you as I suck you off, to come hard in my mouth, pushing my head down forcefully while you ride out your orgasm against my face. But you decide that will have to wait for later. Much later.

Instead you choose to use my mouth for your pleasure in other ways. Your coffee long forgotten, you yank my head back up, grabbing me by the face and squeezing. Rubbing your thumb firmly along my jawline, you tease me by drawing so near to my mouth that it opens wider of its own volition—my tongue reaching for you, pleading for more. You know what power these actions have over me, conscious that when my lips part like that, it means I need you to fill that hole.

And so you do. Inserting just the tip of your first finger initially, making me *really* want it, then, unable to resist, quickly adding your second and plunging deep inside. Fucking my face as I suck you off so exquisitely, groaning at how good it makes you feel to wield such power over me physically, to dominate me psychologically. I want to swallow you whole, opening up the back of my throat so that you can abuse that hole as well. The pads of your fingertips coated in a viscous lube—that which your probing intrusion discovers beneath my uvula. Your cock straining painfully against your boxer trunks—it always catches you a bit off guard just how much harder you get when I open up for you like this, how when you indulge this side of yourself it drops us both into excruciatingly erotic territory. Slippery sounds mixed with little moans escape my mouth, the corners of my eyes tearing up.

These types of noises make you want to really unleash on me. But yet again you decide to wait. Patient, measured, your talent for discipline (in all its many forms) is a thing of beauty. You want to take your time today. So in a split second, you replace your fingers with your tongue, that same fistful of hair guiding me in accordance to your wishes. I kiss you sloppily, ravenously; you can feel how aggressively my need has swelled in such a short amount of time. And you know exactly how to add to my longing while simultaneously giving into it.

You jerk us apart and I begin to whine in protest. Until I see that look in your eye. You bring your lips close to mine again like you're going to give me more of what I wanted. We both know you're not. Because *this* is what *you* want. And now, secretly, it's what *I* want, too. You delight in teasing me this way—drawing your face so near to mine, our points of contact just a hair's breadth away—only to refuse that pleasure, pulling me back just slightly, making me inhale sharply. Your lust hot against my teeth, my heavy exhale penetrating your mouth. You may control the fuck but in moments like these our shared power is most palpable— there's no denying that you need it just as badly as I do—the push and pull elevating our reciprocal ardor. Building up a tension so thick, it clinches the air between us, holding its own, fully inhabiting the space in-between. An energetic exchange so powerful it deserves to be classified as its own form of sex.

"Do you have any idea how hard you make me?"

Words always fail me, most notably in times like these. "Um . . . maybe? Sir?" I falter, unsure of the correct answer.

"Maybe, huh? Well, *maybe* I should show you *exactly* what

you do to me." Not waiting for a response before you begin gloving up my hand.

That perks me right up. "Oh, yes! Yes, please, Sir." Watching you unbutton your jeans does unspeakable things to me.

And I *do* know. How could I not? But I still gasp in delight at just *how* rock hard *and* sopping wet you are when you take hold of my hand and guide it inside, moving my fingers strictly where *you* want them. And then, in an instant, just when I'm *really* starting to enjoy myself, you tear my hand away and it's left painfully wanting. Stripping the glove inside out and tossing it aside, you decide I've had enough. You know yourself too well. If you indulge my touch any longer, we'll end up making this all about you. And right now you've got your sights set on me.

"But . . ." I begin to protest.

"Get up here. I want you over my knee."

There's no arguing with that. "Yes, Sir."

Breathless and quivering, I can't acquiesce quickly enough for my liking. But you're always more patient than me, enjoying how I struggle to find my balance, to come back down to earth long enough to crawl up into your lap. Situating myself just so, I bend over your knees, wriggling my ass just a bit—somewhat in service of the ideal position, in equal parts for your visual benefit.

"You've been *so* good today. I think you deserve a good girl spanking."

"*Ohhhh* . . .Yes, please, Sir." Quickly remembering to express my gratitude, "Thank you, Sir."

You start in on my ass so gently, so lovingly, warming me up gradually, composing a story with your hands across my cheeks, my thighs. Your spankings so exquisite, they're their own art form. Increasing in intensity so infinitesimally that by the time you decide to *really* turn up the heat, I'm not even conscious of how we got from light, rhythmic slaps to thuddy blows in what seemed like the span of only a couple minutes. Or were those hours? Time has fallen away, it has no place here.

Each *thwack* of your palm against my ass lands so heavy, with so much follow-through, it reverberates deep inside my cunt. Spanking as a literal sex act. I start to think I may just come from a beating for the first time when you "accidentally" slip between my thighs. We both know you didn't miss. You never do. Everything you do is careful, precise, perfectly placed.

My cunt is dripping and you needed a taste.

Once there, we both know it's over. Groaning in unison, we know there's no going back.

"Touch yourself for me," you growl.

My left hand can't get to my clit quickly enough.

As you're rubbing your fingers between my lips, marveling at how soaking wet you made me, I begin to play with myself. My clit is still a bit raw from yesterday . . . and the day before. Not to mention the night before that. But no matter, you've got me so on edge, so fucking excited, I can tell that it won't be long. Silently praying that you'll let me come immediately, secretly hoping that you won't, I vacillate between these sharply juxtaposed yearnings within myself. Knowing that you know best, grateful that I don't have to make that decision for myself.

You tease my opening as long as you can stand it; my love of whimpering for more testing the limits of your dwindling will-power. Even a resolve as steeled as yours has a breaking point. But of course it's mine that bends first. I can't take it any longer and the pleading begins to pour out of me.

"Please . . . please . . . *pleeease* . . ."

"Please *what*?" Your tone stern, commanding.

"Please fuck me, Sir. I *need* it. Need you inside me. *Please!* Please do it *now*. My pussy *needs* you. Please! Take me . . . hurt me . . . make me yours . . ."

You can only resist this type of desperation for so long.

As you circle your first two fingers around and around, slicking them up while teasing my hole, one deliciously desperate sound slips out of me that's the end of you—you shove them inside me so fast I cry out. Finding my cunt already so open for you, you brusquely add a third, forcing more screams from me as you thrust deeper. You can tell I'm close already and you're tempted to make this quick and dirty but yet again you rein in your impetuosity. Just . . . . a bit. Instead of fucking me rhythmically and fiercely—with the exact motions that you know will make me come in a matter of minutes (if not seconds)—you decide to pull out of my pussy at an excruciatingly restrained pace.

A long, drawn-out moan that borders on begging cascades over my tongue. I know what's in store for me and my entire body is on high alert awaiting your next move. Pins and needles prickling across the surface of my skin in anticipation. Raking your free hand through my hair to get a *really* good grip, my neck arches back slightly, mouth agape. A sigh accompanies my exhalation as my body relaxes into your hold. I had almost forgotten what your other hand was up to when you slam into me so fast, fluidly, ferociously. Fisting me by the hair while you fuck me at these contradictory speeds—this is the type of torture that is nothing short of agonizing while simultaneously driving me wild. Swollen and growing more sensitive by the second, I rub my clit at a frenzied tempo, spurred by the chaos of salaciousness swirling between us, within me, back into you. Just when you think your cock couldn't possibly ache any more, you feel me tighten around your knuckles.

I struggle to get it out fast enough. "May-I-please-come-for-you, Sir?"

You're torn. Every damn time, part of you wanting to draw out my anguish and ecstasy even longer. But not today. Today your indulgent nature wins. It usually does.

"You may." You continue to thrust in and out of my cunt, swiftly then slowly. "I want you to come *all* over me. I want to *feel* it. Show me *just* how good you can be."

"I'll be *so* good for you . . ." I can barely manage to stumble over the words.

"Yes, that's right. Good girl. *Mmmm . . .*" You feel my cunt begin to pulsate. "That's my good girl."

And that does it. I slip into the abyss and ride my orgasm out across your hand, telling the story of lust and restraint and unfathomable desires.

I WOULDN'T BE THE
SAME WITHOUT HER

Kathleen P. Lamothe

Sometimes a one-night stand can change your life.

I used to think of one-night stands as being good for not much else other than having fun and getting my rocks off . . . that is, until I met her. Her name is Becki, or at least that's the name she gave. I don't even care if it wasn't her real name.

See, I was in a pretty rough spot for a couple years. My daily routine was pretty much like clockwork: wake up hungover, immediately smoke pot to make the aches and pains go away, have a mid-afternoon crossdressing session, feel shame about it, drink to blackout at night. Repeat ad nausem. About once a week or so, just to switch things up, I'd actually concretely contemplate transitioning. And then I'd drink to blackout, smoke pot immediately after waking up, repeat, repeat, repeat.

After years of keeping it private, I finally started challenging myself to bring my crossdressing out of the bedroom. It started slow, but quickly gained momentum. I remember that first night "out," I only walked about half a block, then turned around and bolted it, full tilt, back inside. Which, mind you, is hard to do when you're not used to running in five-inch stilettos. The second night out, about a week after that first venture, I managed to make it all the way to the corner store—not my regular corner store, but the one three blocks away. I didn't want anyone to recognize me while dressed "en femme." But, each time out I did make it further and further. And then of course I would come immediately back home and drink and drink and drink until I passed out.

And so, that was my plan the night I finally mustered up the courage to walk the twenty blocks needed to get me to LIPS, the only dyke bar in town. I must have smoked half a pack on the walk there, what with that nagging voice of self-doubt telling me stop, turn around, *you're a freak, you're ugly, they're all going to laugh at you*, and so on and so on. But I carried on. Once inside, I immediately got myself a drink and found a stool in the darkest recess of the dance floor. Then I sat and tried to make myself invisible. I was fine for the first two or three drinks but then the unease started to mount. I remember at one point scanning across the dance floor and not seeing myself reflected in a single person, despite there being roughly a hundred people of varying gender presentations.

But, in retrospect, how could I have seen myself when I wasn't even sure of how I identified?

That's about the point that my anxiety hit its peak. I put my coat back on, put a smoke between my lips, and bolted for the exit. Just as I reached the door, a woman tapped me on the shoulder and asked, "Excuse me, do you wanna share that smoke with me?"

In those five seconds before I responded, a million excuses as to why I couldn't share it ran through my head—*I'm a germaphobe, I just found out my friend is in the hospital and need to run, it's my only one and I need it for the walk home*—but instead of giving her one of those lines, all that came out of my mouth was an inarticulate, "Uh, sure."

Under the patio lights I got a better look at her. She was quite tall, with broad shoulders, an olive complexion, shoulder length black curly hair with streaks of ginger throughout, and a well-defined jawline. She was quite a bit older than me. I never asked her her age but I'd put us at a good twenty-year age difference. Even though it's now been close to a decade since that night, I can still visualize her outfit to a T. She was wearing a superbly form-fitting black leather corset dress combo, with a red leather cap adorning her head. Mmm. It was my first smell of leather.

"Hey, if our lips are going to be sharing an object so intimately we should at least introduce ourselves, don't you think?" she said with a sly smile, after we had stood there awkwardly for a minute or two. "I'm Becki."

In all my years of crossdressing, both in private and semi-public spaces, I had never come up with a "girl" name; mostly because on an unconscious level, I somehow knew that if I chose a new name than that would make my desires to transition more real, and that was simply way too scary at the time. So in response to her question I simply blurted out the first name that came to my head, "Uh hi, I'm Kyla."

Funny how the name I chose so nonchalantly in that moment became the one I've now used for the past decade of my life.

"Kyla. Wow, what a pretty name. So, listen Kyla. I'm feeling really forward tonight and want to know, what's your favorite color . . . and do you flag it left or right?"

Back then most of my sex life was wrapped up in fuzzy, alcohol-induced states, partly to ease the awkwardness of having to "perform" in the compulsory male role and partly due to me not really knowing or owning my own desires. Nowadays I exclaim with pride that I'm a slutty, perverted bottom, who flags yellow, orange, and black. But suffice it to say, in that moment, I had no idea what she was asking.

"Well, my favorite color is brown, but I'm not really sure what you mean by left or right," I responded, blushing from head to toe.

Becki just about doubled over laughing and said, "Oh honey, it's okay. You know, brown's not really my thing, and I'm pretty sure once I explain the hanky code to you, it won't be yours either. But, whaddya say once this smoke is finished we head back to my place? It's literally just around the corner. Come on; I can explain the code to you on the way."

I was really nervous to go with her because although I had had tons of one-night stands and casual sex, I had never done it while: a) dressed up and using a girl name, and b) relatively sober. At that point in the night, I had only had six drinks in total—three at home, three at the bar—which was a far cry from my typical fifteen-plus before I could even attempt drunken sloppy sex. I honestly think the sober part scared me just slightly more than the dressed as a girl part. But my fears about being a different persona were definitely there, too. In my maniacal web searches for anything trans related, I had seen the remembering our dead website and the trans day of remembrance site—I knew the dangers of not disclosing.

Having smoked the cigarette down to the filter, it was now or never. "Becki, I find you so intriguing, and would like to come back to your place. But there's something I need to tell you before we go. See, I'm transsex . . . uh . . . well . . . I'm transgen . . . well I'm not sure what I am, but I'm definitely trans something." As Becki stood there for a moment, silently contemplating my disclosure, I was thinking about all the right ways to bolt, for the third time that night.

After what felt like an eternity, Becki finally smirked and said, "Oh Kyla, it's all good, I kinda suspected as much." I can still hear the way she said my name.

"And since we're laying everything on the table," Becki

continued, "I guess you should know that technically I'm trans too. I say technically because I was assigned male at birth but I transitioned so long ago now that I don't even really think of myself as trans anymore, just as a woman with a particular kind of history. I often don't even feel the need to tell people, but you seem pretty wound up so I figured that maybe that knowledge would take the pressure off."

And it did. Wow. I was much calmer on the walk to Becki's place. It was only when we got to the entrance of her apartment that I started fretting about what we were going to do and feel in bed. I had yet to sleep with a woman as a woman, with a dyke as a dyke. What did women do together in bed? Would we really scissor? Would Becki, or more importantly I, be able to reinterpret and re-signify my body as female? How would sober-ish sex feel?

"Sorry about the boxes and mess, I'm moving to Chicago for a new position in two days. You'll be pleased to know that I haven't packed up the bed yet though," Becki said with a wicked grin, as she led me hand in hand through her apartment to her bedroom.

Once inside her bedroom, she threw me on the four-post bed and straddled atop of me.

"So, I get the sense that you're not too familiar with kink, but are maybe interested in being shown the ropes, so to speak."

I must have looked sick because I felt as though I was on the verge of both crying and puking and desperate for another drink. So, instead of a coherent yes or no, the best I could do was meow and nod my head vigorously.

"Well, before I tie you up, let's get you out of those clothes, shall we?" Becki started with my thigh-high stiletto boots. She unlaced and removed each boot so delicately, and with such care, that I felt cocooned, warm, and, most importantly, safe.

I find it really cute and adorable to look back on that night, having now lived ten years as an out power bottom. Because I remember the fear and misconceptions I had back then of BDSM. I remember thinking that every top was out to do the meanest, nastiest things to their bottom, regardless of whether the bottom liked it or not. I had no conception, prior to my night with Becki, that, given the right context, things like bondage, spanking, servicing, and piercing, could actually be signs of affection, adoration, and, ultimately, love.

Becki then continued up my body, removing my silver pleather skirt, tight black lace tank top, and red leopard print bra. "Mmm, I like the way you look in just your fishnets and panties. I think I'll let you keep those on . . . for now." And with that, Becki tied me spread-eagle to her bed, taking her time while meticulously fastening each of my appendages.

"So, judging by your 'Well, I'm trans-something' comment back at the bar, I'm guessing that you're not just new to kink, but to transition as well, right?"

Again, I was speechless and could only nod profusely.

"Well, what I want to do with you tonight is actually much less about sadomasochism and more about showing you what a beautiful woman you are. We're going to experiment a little, okay? I want to do things to you that I enjoyed having done to me pre-hormones and pre-surgery and see if they work for you. Understand me?"

Again, I silently nodded.

"Uh-uh, we're doing this together so you're going to have to use your voice. I want you to tell me what's working, what's not, what feels good, what doesn't."

"Yes, I will," I responded short of breath.

A slap on the tops of my thighs.

"Like I said, I don't actually want to hurt you that much tonight, although I'm sure your skin bruises gorgeously. But, when responding you will address me as Ma'am. Anytime you slip up, you get slapped. Understand me?"

My head was reeling. I could still feel my thighs stinging but what I was feeling was way more psychological than physical. Little did I know at the time that that first slap on my thighs was the beginning of oh so much more masochism and servitude.

"Yes, Ma'am," I replied.

"Good, now let's start with your tits. I bet no one's ever called them tits, or breasts, or boobs, before eh?"

"No, Ma'am."

"Oh goodie, I'm honored to be your first. Now, make me wet," Becki said as she shoved her fingers in my mouth. Once they were sufficiently lubed, she started rolling my nipples between her thumbs and index fingers. She started softly, with barely there caresses, and increased the pressure until she was pinching both nipples fairly hard. At that point, I closed my eyes and leaned my head back, reveling in the pain–pleasure dichotomy. Becki then grabbed a fistful of my hair, and forced my head as far down my chest as it would go so that I was staring at my nipples.

"Remember, I said we're doing this together. I'm not going to just let you be a blissed-out pillow-queen. You're going to stay present with me, Kyla. Keep your eyes open and watch what I'm doing to your breasts."

With one hand still gripping my hair, she then bent over and started licking and biting at my nipples, alternating between the two. Again, her biting started lightly and got harder and harder until I was screaming deep moans of satisfaction.

"Oh, so you do like it rough, eh?"

"Yes Ma'am, no one's ever treated my breasts the way you do," I responded very breathily. "Most of my exes have simply treated them as an afterthought."

"Aw, you poor thing. Well, to be honest, I'm ready to explore other parts of your body. But since you enjoy nipple play so much, maybe we can keep them occupied in other ways." Becki said. She reached under her bed and grabbed a set of nipple clamps from her toy box. She screwed each clamp on with the same delicate care that she had shown when removing my boots. Once they were both fastened securely, she took hold of the chain and yanked on it—*hard*. This elicited a scream of pain followed immediately by a rush of euphoria.

"Ooh, I just love the sounds that come out of you. Now, what do you say we get those bottoms off of you? I want you to be completely honest with me, hon. Just how attached to these fishnets and underwear are you? Would you be horrified if I did things to them that would make you never be able to wear them again?" Becki asked. One hand was on the nipple clamp chain and one hand traced a pair of scissors up and down my thigh.

I had that swirling head feeling again. "Uh, well, both the fishnets and the underwear are the first pieces of girl clothes I bought, so I'm definitely attached to them. But maybe fashioning them so that I couldn't actually wear them anymore would give me an excuse to buy some more," I responded with my first undertone of confidence.

More slaps to my thighs, this time about five per, in rapid-fire succession. "Remember? Didn't I say you'd get slapped every time you forgot to call me Ma'am?"

"Yes, Ma'am," I said apologetically.

"So, if I were to make a few little cuts right about here, then you wouldn't mind that much, eh?" she replied as she hooked the scissors under both my fishnets and panties and made little slits in the center. Becki continued to gently cut down the center, the bottom of the scissors lightly grazing my junk as my bottoms were being sliced to shreds. The second I felt the cold hard metal touch my bits, I started shivering profusely.

"Oh, you'll get attention soon enough love, soon enough," Becki said, talking to my genitals as though they were a third lover in bed with us.

Once I was completely naked, Becki positioned herself between my legs, rested her chin on my right thigh, looked up fiercely into my eyes, and said, "So, Ms. Trans-something, do you use specific terms for these bits between your legs?"

God, that was almost too much, actually acknowledging that my genitals existed. I wished I was much more inebriated than I was. The feelings were almost too real, too raw for me to get by sober.

"No, Ma'am. I simply try to ignore the fact that they exist," I responded, with tears welling up under the surface.

"Well, pre-inversion, I used to call mine an enlarged clit, how about we try that for you? I'm going to eat you out now, okay?"

"Yes, Ma'am."

Becki then put a dab of silicone lube on the underside of my clit's head, and sheathed my junk in a black nitrile glove. With two fingers rotating circles on and around the head, she licked up and down the shaft. As my breathing got faster, the pressure on my clit got firmer and firmer, until it sounded like I was hyperventilating. At that point, Becki's tongue joined her fingers and sent me close to the edge of climaxing.

"Don't squirt yet," Becki commanded. "I want you to really ride this orgasm out. Breathe deep. Hold it in. Trust me, it'll feel that much better when I finally let you come."

"Yes, Ma'am. I'll try not to squirt just yet," I responded, with a staccato rhythm to my timbre.

With her mouth and tongue still pressed firmly against my clit, Becki gloved and lubed her hand up and started doing light circles around my butthole. I felt myself on the verge of coming but instead of letting it out, breathed deeply and felt a tingly sensation emanating from my toes to my tonsils. All of this way was so new to me: being treated as a woman in bed, internal orgasms, anal sex . . . it was almost too much.

Almost being the operative word.

After a few minutes of Becki playing with my hole and clit simultaneously, my ass unconsciously loosened. The second that Becki inserted her finger, I screamed out, "Ma'am, I don't think I can hold back from squirting. Please let me come, please, please, please!"

"Hold it in for me just a little longer. Come on, I know you can do it. Just let me work your P-spot a bit, honey," she lovingly demanded, while firmly stroking my prostate. "See, what I've come to realize over the years is that despite all the bullshit that comes with being a woman of trans experience, we are lucky in that, once post-op we get to have both a G-spot and a prostate. Ain't that just the best?"

I didn't know if that was a proper question I needed to answer but didn't want to take my chances at getting slapped again, not at this pure pleasure-filled juncture. So I erred on the side of caution and responded, "Yes Ma'am. We are lucky."

After a few more minutes of her stroking, she finally said the words and allowed me to come. My body shivered and squirmed, as much as it could given the restraints around my limbs. The second I stopped squirting the tears that were earlier held just below the surface started flowing freely. Becki wrapped her arms around my waist and cooed to me as I just bawled and bawled. In contrast to the crying that had sometimes accompanied my mid-day crossdressing sessions though, this was the opposite of shame: this was real release, catharsis, liberation. For the first time that night, I didn't yearn for a drink.

"Oh Kyla, you're so, so, so beautiful. Thank you for letting me go there with you tonight," Becki said, as she untied me from the posts. Once released, both physically and psychologically, she had me drink some water and then just held me silently in her arms, my head resting on her large firm breasts, her hands running through my hair.

After what felt like hours, I finally spoke, choosing my words very carefully, feeling articulate for the first time in ages. "Becki, I've been thinking about transitioning for years. But to me, transsexual has always been a four-letter word. I think you changed that tonight. I don't know where to start though, can you point me in the right direction?"

"Here hon, have one, I stocked up for my move," Becki said, as she handed me a full bottle of Estrace. "I'm not sure if you're aware," she continued, "but according to the newest Harry Benjamin Standards of care for treating trans people, if you're already on hormones when you go see a doctor, their best practice is to continue prescribing them to you."

The very next day I went to my first AA meeting and booked my first appointment with an endocrinologist.

I would not be the same woman I am today without her.

YES MA'AM

K.J. Drake

I'm jittery the whole drive over. I haven't seen Amy in almost a week, and the miles can't pass fast enough. I want to strip off her clothes, wrap my arms around her, and bury my nose in her hair. All week, she's been sending me dirty messages: from the almost tame *I long for you* dashed off in-between customers; to the *I wish I were eating you out right now,* just as I'm crawling into bed; to the *I can't stop thinking about the way you fill me up when you fuck me. Will you do that again soon, please, ma'am?*

Definitely doing that again. Today, if possible. In my bag, I have my favorite lube, both my cocks, and gloves. I probably won't bother with cock or gloves, though. We've been fluid-bonded for a few months, and I want to fuck her with my bare hands, two fingers on her G-spot until she forgets everything but my name.

It's funny, how my cunt tightens every time she calls me "Ma'am." I hate anyone calling me "girl" or "lady" or even any variety of "she." But "Ma'am"? Something about it makes my clit twitch. Every time.

Smiling to myself, I roll down the car window—despite the March chill—so I can casually drape my elbow along the door. It took me a while to find the right outfit, but I figured it out. It's a butch-suave day, a day for a solidly knotted necktie over a sleek, collarless top. The shirt's black, the tie's shot through with gray and purple, the jacket's beat-up pleather, and the jeans are from the men's shelf at the co-op exchange. With the single dangling earring, I look hella queer.

I swing into my usual parking spot and jump out, locking the door as I walk away. In these boots, my swagger's even broader than usual, and I let my arms swing. Then I see Amy, and for a moment, I forget to breathe.

She's coming up the walk from the other direction. Just home from work, and so goddamn gorgeous I don't even have words. Her hair's tousled, her eyes tired, but there's still that fuck 'em edge to her walk.

I want her.

Amy lights up, dropping her bag to pull me in for a kiss. Several. There's the *gods-you're-hot* kiss, the *hello-I-missed-you* kiss, and the *get-your-ass-inside-so-I-can-fuck-you* kiss. One of these days, some bigot's going to yell at us for corrupting the children in public. I don't care.

I pick up her bag, interlace our fingers. "You look beat, babe."

"Work was hell."

"Want to talk about it?"

"No."

Fair enough. I get the door for her. It's her own building, but I like the chivalry. It's a power move, taking her bag and getting the door. Right from the beginning, I'm taking control. I want her spread out underneath me, squirming and begging. I want to take her.

At the stairway, she hangs back, waiting for me to go first. It's a ploy so she can grab my ass. I tell her as much, and she feigns innocence.

Of course, the moment I pass her, she's groping me on the stairwell.

Never been the biggest fan of my own ass (or of the hips that curse me to eternal dressing-room tears) but it's nice to know she appreciates the view.

We pound up the stairs. As I'm fumbling for the key, her mood shifts.

"Beck?"

I turn.

"I'm sorry." She's deflating, anxious and exhausted. "I don't have much in me tonight. It was a long day. I'm sorry."

I push her up against the wall, the exposed brick rough against my fingers. "Amy. Hey. Look at me."

Good, I had her attention.

One hand gripping her neck and the other in her hair, I pull her mouth to mine. My knee's up between her legs, pressing into her. She's mine. I pull back, mere inches between us. "I've got you, Amy. This is all I want from you: your hair wrapped around my fingers, you melting into me. You."

A sigh escapes her. "I want that, Beck. Is that okay?"

"I need you to be mine tonight. My good girl. I want to take care of you."

She nods. "I have to say hi to Samantha."

"Of course." They've been together for years. Amy's my girl, but not *only* my girl. "Say hi to Samantha," I order, releasing her. "Then you're mine."

"Yes, ma'am."

Samantha's in the kitchen when we enter, making dinner with her girlfriend, Lucy. Samantha beelines for Amy. They'll be busy for a few minutes.

I pull off my boots and say hey to Lucy, who's stirring the pot of soup. We kiss hello—we're not dating, but damn, she's a good kisser.

"Hey, do you know where the measuring spoons are?" she says.

"I think they lost them?" I open and close drawers. "Yeah, there's only the tablespoon left. Did you want the quarter-cup measure? Did Amy leave it in her bath salts again?"

"No—yeah, she did, and I found it."

The kitchen's redolent of dinner. "What's cooking?"

"Potato leek soup, with veggie sausage and toast. Do you and Amy want dinner?"

"Later. We've got items on our agenda, first."

She laughs. "Items, or just the one?"

"Just the one," I admit. I look across the room. Amy and Samantha have their arms around each other—no longer kissing, but still entwined. Their dynamic is so different from ours, but I love seeing them together. They're sweet and snarky and comfortable, bickering and making up over the smallest things.

Impulsively, I kiss Lucy again. Her lips are warm and supple. "When are we going to have that threesome?"

She shrugs. "Whenever you want. Not tonight, though. Samantha and I are watching *Brooklyn Nine-Nine*. Send me your schedule?"

"I will."

Just then, Amy and Samantha rejoin us. Samantha winds her arms around Lucy and steals a taste from the soup pot. Amy sidles up beside me. I hook a finger in her belt to drag her closer.

Everyone's talking, something about dinner and work and shitty customers. I don't know, I'm not paying attention. I'm worrying that I'm being selfish, by wanting to top Amy tonight.

Did I misread her signals? Does she want it, too? What if she wants to domme, after all?

Amy nudges me. "Did you want to eat dinner now?"

There's a thread of something plaintive behind her question, unspoken and hopeful.

"I'd rather eat you."

She bites her lip and looks down, then peeks up through her lashes. "Really?"

Yeah, that settles it. She only gives me that look if she wants me to take charge. If I waste time waiting for her to ask, I'll only frustrate both of us. I scoop her up. "You're coming with me."

She grabs my neck, wrapping her legs around my waist.

"Have fun!" says Samantha, looking up from the bread she's slicing. I jerk my chin in acknowledgement.

Amy and I are nearly the same size. It's not the easiest thing, carrying her off to bed like this. I totter through the doorway and pause, letting her reach over my shoulder to lock the door. Just a few steps more.

I tumble her on the bed, sprawl out atop her, and cup her face in my hands. "Hello, love."

"Hey there." Her eyes are shining.

I treasure these moments. All the scattered thoughts that fill my mind are crowded out by her presence. Between her eyes and mine is an almost tangible space, warm and safe. How did I ever get this lucky? How was I given the right to hold her down? She's strong, wise, beautiful, and I still go speechless when she enters a room.

It's not that I'm the dominant one. She's sharply opinionated, and ready to fight for her beliefs. When we disagree—and we do—she's no pushover. We argue. Sometimes we convince each other. Sometimes we grudgingly accept that both of us have good reasons. And she tops me just as often as I top her. When I'm exhausted, she strokes my hair and holds me close. When I'm small and subby, she dommes me with a ferocity that thrills me from the inside out.

Despite that fierce strength, she yields to me. On days when she's small and anxious, she spreads herself open and lets me take her. I'm honored that she trusts me, and I love her for it.

She's noticed my distraction. Her adoring look shifts, and takes on a questioning cast.

I respond with solidity, stability. *I've got you, babe.* I rub my thumbs behind her ears, twine my fingers through her hair, and hold tight.

She melts, mouth falling open.

Slowly, I kiss her. I'm holding her face between my palms and tasting her deeply. She's sweet and fresh, mouth wet with arousal, and I want more.

I release her hair and run my thumbs over her jaw, searching out the nerves that lie here, between skin and bone.

"Mmm, that feels good."

I search out her reactions, fingertips exploring for new sensations. Thumbs on her neck, I press into the tender flesh, listening to her hum of pleasure, watching her minutely for any flicker. Her eyes glaze over, and then close.

Hastily, I release my grip.

"I went a little fuzzy," she says. "I could have passed out."

"I'm sorry."

"No, it felt good," she says. "I would have let you."

She would. That's what worries me.

"I felt so safe." She stretches, languorous.

"You are, my love. I've got you," I answer. I want her to trust me, to relax into me, to not worry. That's why I have to watch, and worry, and let go before she passes out.

I'm tired of not being able to see her tits, so I pull her shirt off. While I'm at it, I strip off the rest of her clothes. Mine, too.

She has the greatest tits. They're just the right size for squeezing: perky, soft, and delicious. Her skin, too, is warm and kissable. I lick long, spiraling circles around her nipples until she's arching toward my mouth. Then I latch on and suck hard, grinning at her squeak of surprise.

Her hands are loose on the bed. Unrestrained. She's holding them up by her shoulders, exactly where they'd be if I were holding her down. Coyly, she looks at me. Not asking outright. Just letting me notice, and waiting.

Of course I won't disappoint. I seize her wrists and put my weight on them.

She fights back. Not hard, just making sure I mean it.

I hold her down.

When she's tested her restraints, she relaxes. "Thank you," she breathes.

For answer, I pepper her tits with kisses and lick mercilessly down her ticklish sides until she's writhing and shrieks "Yellow!"

Instantly, I stop and let her breathe. That's a safeword, a *slow-down!* signal. I rest my cheek on her thigh, still holding her wrists in my hands. From here, her dick is in easy reach of my mouth, and I reach out to kiss the tip.

I've been low-key looking forward to eating her out all day. Now, though, I prolong the anticipation, dropping kisses along her thighs, mouthing the tenderest bits of skin with my lips. At last I take her all the way into my mouth: still a little soft, intimately warm, and so, so satisfying.

"Oh, fuck, Beck. That's so good."

It is. Down in my cunt, I can feel myself getting wetter. I pull her deeper, swirling my tongue around her clit and sucking hard. For a moment, my whole world narrows to this: her dick in my mouth and her wrists in my hands. I slide back and forth, relishing in the glide of cobweb-soft skin across spit-drenched lips.

I pull away just long enough to order, "Put your hands behind your head." I want her restrained, I want my hands free, and I don't have the patience for ropes. She complies, and I resume my back-and-forth, eliciting another groan of pleasure from her. She's getting worked up, muscles bunching under her skin as she tries to hold still.

I dip my mouth lower, spreading her open with both hands. Her hole is salty-sweet, clean and tangy under my tongue. I think my cunt is dripping—actually dripping—on the bed. I lap at her, circling her hole, teasing her, feeling the tight muscles start to give. Above my head, she swears softly.

"Fuck. Fuck, yes, Beck, that's—really lovely. Yes, please. Please, Beck?"

I press my tongue into her, teasing slowly, until she's begging me to fuck her.

Then there's the awkward moment when I pull away and lean over her, trying to reach the bottle next to the bed. There's no ideal time for this ritual pause, and her voice is edgy when she asks, "Where're you going?"

"Just grabbing the lube."

Amy bites her lip, watching me slick up my fingers. She's sprawled out on the bed. Again, I'm momentarily breathless with her beauty. I love seeing her like this: legs wide, hips canted up, arms akimbo, hands trapped behind her head. She looks away—nerves? self-consciousness?

"Look at me." I keep my voice low. Intimate.

Her eyes snap back to mine.

I nod, trying to convey how utterly focused on her I am. "You're making me all wet," I say, for distraction.

"Really?"

"Mm-hm." I slide my free hand down past my belly and slip two fingers in my cunt. A breathy sound escapes me: my clit is swollen hard and aching for touch. "Look, baby. Look what you do to me." I show her my hand, pushing both fingers into her mouth.

She sucks immediately, eyes closing, tongue warming my perpetually cold fingers.

I push deeper, fucking her mouth. "I love taking you, Amy." Mouth, dick, ass—I like touching every inch of her, letting her feel used and controlled and cherished. I graze a fingertip across her hole, where a few minutes ago I relentlessly devoured her.

She whimpers, tilting her hips up, trying to get me inside her.

"Not yet, baby." I pull my hand from her mouth and wipe it across her tits, all the while keeping up my insistent teasing of her hole.

"Please?" she whispers. "Please."

The smallest fingertip, just a centimeter of entrance. Tiny movements, barely more than a flutter. I lean forward, slipping my free hand under her neck, touching my forehead to hers.

"Are you going to fuck me?" She's plaintive, now, antsy.

"Yes, love. I'm fucking you right now."

"I want you to fuck me *hard*." There's an edge of petulance in her voice, lined with frustration.

I can't tease her too long, or she'll give up. "I know, baby. I know. I've got you." I caress her tits, her arms, her hips, trying to distract her as I slowly work her open.

At last, I slip all the way in.

Amy sighs with long-delayed relief. When I slide back, though, she winces. "More lube?"

Carefully, I pull out. The bottle's slippery with drips, and the lube is cold on my fingers. I swirl it around, one-handed, warming it with my skin. Then I ease back inside. "Better?"

She nods, eyes closing.

I find her G-spot, textured and appealing, and press against it.

Not too hard—she's not fully warmed up yet—just a crooking of my finger, a brush of fingertip against sensitive walls.

She squirms and whimpers deliciously. Good. I want her begging for more, not flinching away. Slowly, I massage her walls, teasing her spot, feeling her open up around me.

When I settle into the circling rhythm that she loves, it's as if she comes apart at the seams, turning boneless and babbling: "Yes, yes, yes, that, that, yes please, ohhh, more of that."

Satisfaction warms me. Soon, I'll make her come. I love this, the way she's spread out before me, my hand inside her, her eyes squeezed shut in pleasure.

I lean forward for a better angle, splaying my free hand on her sternum. I'm fucking her harder now, two fingers circling her G-spot, feeling her contract around me.

Her eyes open, suddenly distracted. "Beck? Am I allowed to come?"

I raise one eyebrow and thrust harder into her. "Do you have a choice?"

She shakes her head.

Sometimes she worries that her pleasure is an imposition, something selfish. So I take the decision away from her. I like to tell her she's not allowed to think about that. She's close to an orgasm, and I don't intend to let up. "I'm not going to stop, baby. I'm going to make you come. Say my name when you do."

She's panting. "Okay."

My arm's tiring, but I don't care. Clearly, I haven't fucked her often enough. For a split second, I shift to a better angle, and then?

Then—I—fuck—her.

Hard, deep, fast, all the finger strength I have. It's not long before she's shattering, babbling my name in an incoherent stream.

"Fuck, fuck, *fuck* yes don't stop yes please Beck, please Beck I'm coming, I'm coming Beck, Beck Beck Beck—"

She's crashing over the edge. I ease up, and still. She looks utterly spent, eyes closed, traces of a grimace lining her face.

"Deep breath, love," I tell her.

Shakily, she inhales.

I slide out of her as gently as I can, mindful that her every nerve is firing. Then I'm out. I'm tugging the towel out from under her, wiping my hands and tossing it aside. I'm pulling the blanket over us and sliding my arm under her. She's still shaking with after-shocks, but curls into me.

We lie like that for a long time, in blissful silence. My clit aches. In a few minutes, I'll make her fuck me. Maybe I'll hold her by the hair while she eats me out. Maybe I'll grab her hand and use her fingers to fuck my cunt. Or both—her mouth on my clit, her fingers deep inside me, until an orgasm washes over me.

Soon, but not yet. I squeeze her tight, hoping she understands what I lack the words to say.

She clings to me. "Beck . . ." is all she says.

Sometimes, that's all we need.

THE ESTRANGED

G.B. Lindsey

"Sit," I said, because what else was I supposed to do? But it's late now and she's sitting at my kitchen table, smelling of gardenia, and I'm regretting it.

It's hot. The air is thick as pudding. Shine's black pumps look foolish at the ends of her legs. Her legs really do go on forever. She dallies a fingertip in the bowl of blueberries. "So I hear you're gray-ace now."

My ears buzz and buzz, and the skin of my mouth goes tight. I drop the knife onto the cutting board and turn on her.

Shine flinches. Her hands fly up. "Sorry, I'm sorry, not 'now.'"

"Fuck you."

"Rona," Shine pleads.

I point a finger at her head like a stage actor. But there's nothing to say, nothing I haven't just said. Insults are currency. The more there are, the less they're worth, and the faster they blow down the gutter.

I start cutting the carrots again, my pulse cacophonous. Every carrot in this apartment will be in particles by the time this ends.

Shine is long and beautiful, her hair is long, her eyelashes are long, her thumbs are longer than her pinkies. I stare at her hands, those fingers clenched tight around each other like she's praying, and wonder how deep the knife will go when I inevitably chop into my own finger.

Would she call for help? Would she just run out of here, as far from the injury as she can get?

It's unfair to think it of her. There was a time when the idea of her not helping me would have had me laughing. "Why did you come here?"

"Why did you open the door?" she snaps back.

I slap the knife onto the cutting board again. "Because there's a Halloween sign covering my peephole."

The hurt twists her face. I want to laugh at her. "Oh, don't, Shine. Don't look at me like that."

She schools it away. She might be before a camera. Maybe this is all just one of her movie scripts, and I refuse to learn my part.

What kind of a name is Shine anyway?

Oh, you know. It's my name.

It's a nickname, is what it is. It's our baby and she got custody. It's a stupid name.

It was *my* name for her.

She sighs. "I don't know any other way to look at you."

Then don't look at all. But her eyes feel like twin weights settling back into grooves: a pile of blankets over my body on the night the season turns, the heft of a cat settled on my chest. I still want her to look at me.

It's the middle of August, and no delta breezes. The stifling night has followed her inside. The hair along her brow is damp with sweat, and her throat shimmers. She'd folded down into my kitchen chair like it had been made to cradle her. I got that chair after she left; she had no right to sink into it like that, to cross her legs and sway her knees, pull her skirt against her skin just so, prop her elbow by the blueberries. She had no right to interrupt my dinner, to see the dishes neglected in the sink. She has no right to be here.

This matters exactly nil to the tangle in my head. "Why *are* you here?"

"I was in town." Shine sits on the chair's edge, fingers curled over her knees. They are bare and knobby, the visible inch of her thigh imprinted by the sequins on her skirt. "I wanted to see you."

"After three years."

Shine kneads her forehead. I wonder if her headaches still get to her, a small knife punching through tender tissue. She used to throw up. She used to lie in bed naked, chest huffing and falling, because touch was a trigger and even clothing hurt.

She liked ice, though, just behind her ears.

"Has it been three years?" she drones at her palm.

I put down the knife again. "Yes. Three years." How, *how* does one not count? A little clock had wedged under my diaphragm the moment she exited my life, ticking, dragging minute after minute between us like cement slabs.

"How's France?" I spit.

"Oh, here we go."

"No, I really want to know."

She snorts. "It's French, okay?"

"This is what I always liked about us, how we could talk about anything."

Her headshake is different now, her face withdrawn. "Don't. Don't do that."

"I'm telling you how I feel." Like I did then, but you can bet I won't be doing it anymore. There are doors I won't open for her, doors she used to sail right through.

"You're still so *angry*." She says it like a surprise, more to herself than to me, and that's what holds the inferno back, snuffs the explosion. She looks at her hands, her eyes wide, distant. I don't want her to look like that, like she doesn't recognize things the way she should.

"You did some infuriating things," I say at last. I am angry today. Not every day. The smell of her slinks through the kitchen. I haven't smelled her here in years. Her pillowcase smelled just like this for a week before I washed it.

"What, leaving?"

"Not answering my calls."

"I answered!"

"Two sentences! *Two sentences.* You gave me a fucking party line, Shine."

Her fury has always lit her eyes from beneath. "And you went off, just like I knew you would. I didn't see the point after that."

"So it was a test?" A silent ultimatum?

"Yes."

The way lovers test each other, the way women punish. "Great."

"*No*, Rona. Shit. It wasn't a test." She shakes her head and her hair drifts. A second goes by. "Sometimes I think it was."

And sometimes I think I was wrong, what I did. Sometimes I know it. Those are dark days.

"We were friends. We agreed to talk this time." When we didn't talk, history taught, everything cascaded, piled in heaps at the bottom of the slope, buried the ley lines between us.

"I was busy!" She slaps her chest, emphasizing words. "I had commitments, same as you. You knew I was in auditions."

"You didn't tell me you were moving to Europe until you were nearly out the door."

The pause is ominous.

"We were not together then," she says slowly, color in her cheeks. Her eyes are dark and sharp and I used to love it when she was angry, but not when she was angry with me. "You didn't get any say over where I went or who I went with."

"There was a who?" I ask the carrots.

She deflates. "Not then."

But there has been since. There hasn't been for me. She was always better at that, offering her heart.

I used to want to know about them. Now, what does it matter?

She stands. She's vibrating. "You don't get to be angry at me for making a decision about my life."

I shake my head. "Why are you dressed like this?" Like she's going to a cocktail party. Is this French, too?

She dashes it away. "You do not get to be angry. They were my plans. You were not entitled to my plans."

But you were my first. Even as friends, that didn't change. There's nothing I can say out loud. I said plenty, years ago. I felt right, then. I've thought about it for three years, though, and the light changes. The way it falls upon angles, what it illuminates.

Mostly, she's just been gone. That hole's edges are still raw.

"I just wanted to know." My voice is hoarse. There are fires up the valley, there's dust and ash in the air. I wipe my mouth. "We were going to tell each other things."

Her sigh sounds as old as I feel. "I wasn't trying to hurt you. I just . . . didn't know how to tell you."

"Text. Email. A phone call."

"Which I did."

"Barely."

"We have *talked* about that part," she says, too fast, and sits down again with a thump. "We talked about it, just now."

"And that's supposed to make it go away?"

"*No,* I just—" She rubs her forehead, two fingers pressing tight to her brow.

"We were friends. I still think we are, sometimes."

So do I. But. "Friends who don't talk?"

"Can we please not fight about this?"

There was a time I would have considered her headache first, would have stepped off the raft before it bashed itself on the rocks. "No."

"I'm sorry," Shine whimpers, her fingers plowing into her temples now, and suddenly the raft is outbound again and I am stepping off it. I open the freezer and find the green beans.

"Here." When I press them to her nape, she sighs from her toes. Her body tilts back into my hand. I hear the *grnt-grnt* of her teeth and push my thumb into the hinge of her jaw.

She nudges my hand away, but opens her mouth and lets it hang, and her teeth don't grind anymore.

"Should have written you." Her words slur.

Arguing is like trying to shove this August night away, when all anyone wants is to lie on the linoleum naked with the lights off. I'm just not angry anymore.

"Doesn't matter now," I say, and her eyes flicker wide. She tilts upright, staring at me like I've punched her.

"It doesn't?"

"It doesn't." It might be a lie, tomorrow. Last week I muttered at my cupboards for half an hour while abusing pasta, scalding plates. The week before that, I rewrote my caustic emails in my head, all the things that would have said it better, that would have saved us.

Today I would have thought, *it's okay to call.*

"I'll let it go," I mutter. It's tricky, this promise. Tacky like the heat, but it never stays where you stick it. "I'm not mad."

"You are." There's a certain horror in her tone, ages stretching before her and this permanently paving the road she'll walk down.

"Then I'll stop being mad." I dump the knife in the sink. It clanks like a dish breaking. "I can do that. We did it before."

Another foul up, another teaching moment. That time, she had let me back in. This time, it's my turn. But there have to be boundaries. "This." Whatever this heat, this weight, this gnarled knot winding between us is. "It doesn't work—"

"It worked!"

"It doesn't *last*," I correct, and she falls silent.

Did I ever tell her how, from the very first day, she'd lodged in my throat? How she hung in my chest and draped my shoulders, and I didn't have a word for it, not love or lust, just a closeness that held all my points and pieces together, flared dark and sweet in my guts, clicked home like a bolt? No, I never said those words. I should have. "Maybe it's just not meant to be."

"I *love* you." She sounds broken.

My heart shakes. "Yeah, when I don't love you. And when I do, you don't." On and on for years, until we both didn't, and then we both did.

And then. *Our* two years. Finally, alignment. Finally she was mine and I was hers. Her clothes mixed with mine, I cooked pork tacos while she sang along to Florence, she tasted like berries on Sunday mornings and full fat cream in the winter. We lay on the carpet and read badly written books out loud until we hurt from laughing. I went to her screenings. We tucked atop each other in our bed, rubbed unshaven legs together, kicked the blankets to the floor in our fervor and kept as quiet as we could when the windows were open because the courtyard echoed even a whisper.

By the end, I was published, touring conventions, and she was gone on weekends, had an agent down south. We were apart more than we were together. Being in love was a gentle simmer; we could smile at each other like dusk falling. We could forget to call every night, forget how it felt to wake up to each other.

We could call it quits, for the job, for the opportunity. For now. She'd looked gorgeous in her movie, when I finally found the stomach to watch it. The French Riviera behind her, her costar standing with her in the rain, her slouched silhouette backed by the golden sea and her sandals dropping into the surf.

The counter blurs. I should finish the carrots. Where's the knife?

"Do you love me now?" she asks.

Always. Never. Define love. I don't answer. I stare at my cutting board and I stay silent.

"Okay." I hear her stand up, smooth her skirt. Her car keys rattle on the table and I know her hands are shaking. "Okay."

I can't let her go. I'll never see her again, except on floor-to-ceiling screens, in Technicolor. They never get her eyes right, never the molasses-slow bleed of brown into gold. Strain makes me harsh. "If you'd just called me—"

"Did you want me to?" she cries, hands in fists. I step back, and she pulls at her hair, derailing the bun—an intentional mess, perfected by an hour in front of the mirror—atop her head. She swears at it when her nail snags. "Why would you talk to me when I, for two *years*—"

"What? For what two years?" Our two years?

She lifts her hands and drops them, twice. "Rona."

"What?"

She waves at me, herself, all around the kitchen and the hall beyond. I still don't know what she's talking about. It occurs to me that I almost moved away this past summer, and if I had, she would have showed up at the door and found someone else here, and wouldn't have known where to find me.

"I liked sex. Like, all the time." Her face is blotching up. She sounds miserable. "And you're gray."

"Whoa." I forget the cutting board, the carrots. "Whoa, stop."

Tears cloud her eyes. "You never told me you didn't want it."

I've seen her like this, jittery, when her grandmother went to the hospital, when a director threatened a job. When despite her best efforts, things refused to flow. The last night I can remember was rushed but not unfeeling, and she touched me with her mouth and suckled me into a white haze.

"Oh my God." I want to touch her hair. "Is that why you never called me after?"

"You never called *me*." Her petulance flounders under the tears. I give up and pull her to me. She pushes back and I let her go.

"I don't want this to be—" She stops. "This needs to not be angry."

"I'm not angry."

She shakes her head.

"Do I look angry?"

"You never look angry, don't you get it? You hide it, even from me."

How do I tell her that I have to? Anger means fighting, means we're not working. It's stupid. People fight. They stay together. But when I fight, I feel so sick and wrong after, I think all night about the things I said and the ways I cut her, and it's different.

"We were ending." Even the friendship had been eroding by then. I can't keep the cracks out of my voice. "You weren't talking to me."

"I was busy," she whimpers, "I had to leave and I didn't know how to tell you."

"I thought you'd be mad. If I pushed."

"Well, you should have pushed!"

"You didn't like it when I did!"

"You're stupid." She yanks a fistful of my shirt. "God. You think I couldn't get over that?"

"Thanks," I say, and then she's kissing me.

Her lips are chapped but her mouth is soft, and her breath hitches. And then she's away. "Fuck, I'm sorry."

I pull her back in, irritated. "Don't apologize."

"I'll damn well apologize if it's something you don't want to do."

"I want to do it!" I always wanted to do it, with her. She stares at me like a startled cat, so I keep going. "I never didn't want to do it with you."

"But." She waves her hand. I catch it, tuck it between us. "*All* those times?"

She taught me everything. She let me touch her, let me learn. "I can't remember one where I wasn't on board."

"Okay?" she says, like she can't believe it.

"*You're* stupid." It's all I can think of. She smiles, red cheeks, damp eyes. Her laugh is clogged and pitiful against my mouth.

We still fit. Our mouths, the curve of her fingers into my palm, and she smells . . . "You never changed your perfume."

"Tonight, I didn't." She nearly asks it, like she's waiting to be struck. I see her standing in front of some hotel mirror, winding up her hair, dabbing the perfume she knows I'll recognize against her throat, and it's impossible not to kiss her, to lunge in full bodied. She lets out a kicked sound. Her arms go slack around my neck, fingers threading into my hair. I back her out of the kitchen into the hall, into the bedroom, and the blinds are all open, the lights are on, at night my apartment is a fishbowl and here we are, plastered together for all the world to see.

I hit the wall, the wall, finally the switch, and the room goes streetlight yellow. She inhales, sharp, almost searing, and I have one thought: I'm going to show her how I always want her.

"Rona?" Her hands leave me and I feel her unsnapping, unzipping, hesitating. She drops the dress like a rag and stumbles out of it, back into my arms, pushes down white cotton panties, and she's naked except for her pumps. Then those are off too, and she's shorter than me again. The smell of flowers thickens.

Under her arms, under her breasts. She put it everywhere, she may have even put it between her legs. I imagine her trembling in front of the mirror, cursing herself for hoping, for thinking anything would come of it but doing it anyway because what did she have to lose?

When she goes down onto the bed, it's a clumsy slide, onto her back with her legs fixing me between. She's hot and damp in the cradle of her pelvis, the hair grown thick. She isn't one to wax, to care how it all looks. The stretch of her bare hip, the crease of her thigh and the round of her buttocks feel endless. She shivers when I hitch her into me.

It used to be clinical with her. I could search my way through. Watch her muscles twitch and ripple, and for a while I thought I was strange. Removed. How could I not lose myself entirely in the length of her like everybody said I should, the shadowed curves and the moist pockets? How could I *think* this through?

She trembles in the same way when I touch the inside of her. Her legs squeeze solid at my hips, and I still have my jeans on, so I push down, roll into her slow, and she jerks at the roughness where she is bare and open.

She's wet, her arms goose-pimply. The smell of her on me is thick.

"I want to be in you," I whisper to her temple. Slick and hot, fluttery with muscle, fingers pressed deep, thumbs smothered in foggy folds. Sometimes the two of us splayed wide and pushed up against each other, rubbing and swollen, wet and *wet* until we came, and our breathing went hectic and her ribs dug into mine with each heave. But I never really meant fingers or thumbs. I wanted to be *in* her, wrapped up in her narrowed eyes and her snorty laugh. I have always wanted to know her and for her to know me. Sex was a means to climb further inside, sex was messy and incidental, and with her, it was muddling, heavy, good because she was on the other side of it. Sex meant she was climbing into me, too.

"I want this because you want it." The words are ungainly in my mouth. "I *like* doing this to you."

I roll her breasts up and back down. They're so small and plump, the areolas sloping oval, and they haven't changed at all. She pushes into my palms. I nip the underside of one because I know she likes it, and her nails scrape my scalp. She swallows, chokes out, "But do you like it for you," no question mark at the end, too unhinged for that. I nod into the skin between her breasts.

She shoves my pants down then, so roughly it burns. I've never been as small as her; more curve, more fat. She digs fingers into my thighs. I feel her pushing the blood away, white bands. She slides inward and thumbs my clit and I shudder into a heap over her.

"Not yet," I manage. Her first. She keeps rubbing, though, relentless circles that jolt my spine, pushing up each time, up, up. Her stare is relentless. Heat roars like an engine. I back off and her head comes off the pillow with a broken yelp. Her breath gets even faster; she drags the shirt over my head.

She likes breasts. She told me about mine once, tired and garbled with her foot dangling off the bed. She said mine were large, pretty, that she was indifferent about her own. I like hers. They almost disappear when she's lying on her back. Her nipples are dark and sensitive.

She can't come from them alone, though. I push three fingers into her and up top, she stills as though I shocked her. Her hips, though, flex over and over. She quivers inside and I've always loved that. A thumb on her, pressing firm, makes her swear. Her leg becomes a vise around my waist, calf sweaty, hitching higher. She plunders my mouth, and most of it is breath and broken sound, but I kiss her when I can. It's hard to concentrate, to work her the way I remember. The way she's moving, though, maybe it doesn't matter.

"If I licked you," she gasps, lets it end there, but it doesn't end for me. I remember her head ducked between my legs, nails a soothing scritch on each thigh, holding me wide, her tongue a broad, flat heat over my hole, and orgasm nearly bulls through me. I duck away, fight it back. She moans like the idea hurts. "No, I want you to come, I want—"

"Doesn't mean I don't like it," I rasp, needing her to understand, "if I don't come, it doesn't—"

"Okay," she nods, "okay," and squeezes my fingers inside her. She cradles my face and kisses me so deep. She likes it deep, I remember, so I get my arm under her and I lift her onto my lap, and it's not graceful but when she comes down, her grunt cracks from her like a sob, most of my hand in her now. She circles her hips once, and then breaks in a wave of gasps; she bucks and bucks, face buried in my shoulder. I work her with my thumb until she whines, until her teeth pinch my skin. Her sweat is salty and slick, her hand seized over my breast.

We end up side by side, breathing hard. The bed is cramped, the ceiling a blur. Outside, a car goes by. The scent of gardenia clings.

"I'm not just in town." Her voice is drunk. "I'm *here*."

My throat locks up. "For good?"

She takes a breath. "If you want?"

I want.

OWNING A COCK

Amy Butcher

I dream of a cock
like a cartoon frog's tongue
a long spiral of pink flesh
that unfurls as if slung

This cock of my dreams
this party-noise-maker
it crinkles and crackles
it snaps outward—no faker

It tickles your clit
and rolls into your cunt
then snaps back to mine
completing its stunt

I shake myself awake, slowly pulling myself back from this rhyming wet dream. I wonder if Good Vibrations might have this cock—this acrobatic cock—already in stock.

Lucky for me
There's so many they hawk
Pink, blue, and green . . .
the rainbow is mine.
Cocks in all sizes,
From petite to bovine.

I stretch again and yawn, trying harder to pull myself into consciousness, letting go of the rhymes even as my brain still lingers, stroking the memory of all the cocks I've ever seen on display.

There were the huge ones, shaped like the forearm of a young boy reaching for puberty. Dolphin-shaped ones that would surely be as helpful to me as Flipper ever was to Porter and Sandy. Cyber-cocks, square where things should never have edges, that reminded me of a children's toy where the square wooden peg never fit into the round hole. There were even realistic ones—veined, circumcised, and oddly erect—built as if to replace one that had somehow been lost somewhere between conception and now.

I sit up and run fingers through my unruly hair, hoping to scratch my brain back into this reality. You remain curled beside me in bed, back towards me, snoring quietly.

I know I could pick a cock that would be nothing but a tease for you, bulging out the crotch of my jeans, extending slightly down my left thigh, but with the promise of machismo unrealizable.

Or I could pick a Viagra cock, always erect, ready and reporting for duty.

Or I could choose an ambivalent cock, the magic of the malleable steel inside giving me choice: hedge my bets . . . or strut my stuff by bending it fully erect and putting my money where my mouth is—or really where I hope your mouth will be.

Even as I swing my feet towards the floor, I know that after the choice of cock has been made, another choice still remains. I must decide how best to attach this implement to my own body.

If I'm simply packing, then tucking Mr. Softy into my boy shorts will do. But if I want to be able to drive this thing, then a full leather harness is the gold standard. One strap like a thong or two like a jockstrap, I leave that up to you. Flat nylon webbing is always an option—a good choice for vegans but still an environmentally conflicted one—yet, no matter what anyone says I'm telling you these things are just not sexy. If I've been doing my Kegel's, there is even the "hold inside" double dildo requiring no harness at all, but this biological invasion seems unbecoming to this "fella."

Once cock and harness are secure, there remains one final attachment to be formed: the imaginal. For imagination is the true wielder of this device and building that attachment takes time.

I slip off the side of the bed, and stand to pull on an old sweatshirt. You exhale fully, rattling lips, and pull the covers tight, sinking deeper into sleep. Sliding into well-worn slippers, I shuffle into the kitchen to make coffee.

Early on in our relationship, I can remember nights when I would strap on the cock we bought together, the one that fit you perfectly, nights that would leave me feeling like a clumsy-cock. I would climb on top of you, spreading your thighs wide, hungry to find my way inside. It might take some guidance from your hand or mine to find the entry—the feedback systems on these things are so dull—but once inside, I would try to measure the pulse of my hips to match the length of that cock, hoping to avoid that awkward moment of premature withdrawal, that horrible moment when my thrust would be deflected because I had pulled back too far and popped out, leaving me lost and confused like a small child waiting for someone to guide me back home.

Once back inside, you would squeeze around my shaft, trying to pleasure me in the ways you'd learned from your past experience with fleshy cocks. But this just made me feel like an autistic-cock, a cock that couldn't connect to the outside world, that couldn't feel your ministrations. And even when you moaned in pleasure I doubted, feeling like an atheist-cock, a cock that would not believe in your lusty cries as proof of the power of this disconnected extension of me.

They say a transplanted sapling takes time to extend new roots, so too a strapped-on cock requires experience before the tentacles of imagination can slowly spiral from the silicon back into the soul.

I could feel those tentacles grow the first time you gave me a blow job. I stood, legs splayed, looking down over the curve of my belly to your hooded eyes. You looked back up at me directly, taking the whole of my opalescent silicon blueness into your mouth. Part of me wanted to grab hard onto your hair and shove the implement deep into the back of your throat, but an empathetic gag reflex held me back. Good thing, too, because if I had, then I would have missed the sight of your mouth pulling back along my shaft, your tongue teasing slowly at the tip, circumnavigating it then pulling a tenuous line of spit out between us both. I would have missed that magic moment when you crawled your way back along that saliva mooring line, closed your eyes and wrapped your soft lips back around me once again. I would have missed that moment when the separation between my clit, this cock, and your mouth all but disappeared.

I could feel those imaginal roots grow deeper still each time you straddled me, plunging yourself down again and again onto my bucking cock. The wet slapping sound of your pussy meeting my shaft, the feel of my palm splayed across the damp, sweaty heat between your breasts—supporting you—while the other hand teased at your nipples, pinching and forcing you back in an arch of pain and delight.

These experiences fed me, rooted me, over and over, until one day I realized—to my complete surprise—that I was finally fucking you with nothing but my imagination. The silicone and leather had become iconic, space holders for an energy that drew up through my tail, coiled inside my pelvis, unfolded out and through you, pushing you into a pleasure you did not know you had demanded, making me come . . . come into a power I did not know I possessed.

I pour a cup of the steaming fresh coffee and sip, almost awake now.

I smile, savoring the memories, certain in the knowledge that now, I fully own my cock.

ABOUT THE AUTHORS

MARY P. BURNS is a long-time resident of New York City. She received a Master of Fine Arts in Playwriting from Columbia University in 1991, after which the muses departed for points unknown, leaving no forwarding address, so she carved out a career as an executive assistant. When happenstance left her with the opportunity for some major time off, she sharpened her pencils and hoped for the best. Luckily, the muses returned, and she hasn't stopped writing since. Her first novel, *Forging a Desire Line,* was published by Bold Strokes Books in May 2020. You can reach her at maryburns11C@gmail.com.

AMY BUTCHER is a writer, artist, bodyworker, business consultant, and liminal guide who lives and works in San Francisco. Her award-winning novel *Paws for Consideration* was published in 2012. Her short story "Touched" appeared in *Best Lesbian Erotica 2012.* Follow her many adventures at www.amybutcher.com.

ANITA CASSIDY is a bisexual, poly, and kinky writer as well as a mother of two, sister, niece, friend, and partner. Living in London, she runs a conscious relationship community and hopes, with her work, to engage people with the idea of change and awareness as well as normalizing all forms of consensual sexual expression.

RAIN DEGREY (she/her) is a writer, advice columnist, podcaster, and educator who has been performing and teaching for the past decade. Her work has taken her from Kink.com to Harvard University, and many places in between. Demystified sex education is one of her greatest passions. For more information go to www.raindegrey.com.

KIKI DELOVELY (kikidelovely.wordpress.com) is a kinky, witchy, non-binary femme who moonlights as an erotica writer when she's not helping others through energetic healing or spiritual coaching. Their work has appeared in dozens of publications, including *Getting It: Female Sexual Agency, The Sexy Librarian's Dirty 30, Vol. 3*, and *Corrupted: Erotic Romance for the Modern Age*. Kiki strives toward erotica that reads as fine literature and connects us with our highest selves.

K.J. DRAKE is a genderqueer writer dyke who lives in Chicagoland. When not writing queer fiction, they like making out with their partners, walking through the prairie, and ruminating. They can be found on Twitter @nerdwen.

NICOLE FIELD writes across the spectrum of sexuality and gender identity. She lives in Melbourne with one of her partners, two cats, a whole lot of books, and a bottomless cup of tea. She can be found on Wordpress: nicolefieldwrites.wordpress.com and Twitter: @faerywhimsy.

HEART is a smart-ass with a sweet ass. Canadian, queer, kinky, switchy, witchy, ethically non-monogamous, fairly anxious, forever crushing, usually blushing, she writes to remember how it felt. You can follow her adventures on Patreon @herdirtylittleheart, or check out more of her writing at ZeroSpaces.com.

TOBI HILL-MEYER is an indigenous chicana trans woman with fifteen years experience working in nonprofits, serving on boards, and consulting in nonprofit management. She is editor of the Lambda Literary Finalist anthology *Nerve Endings: The New Trans Erotic*, author of children's books *A Princess of Great Daring* and *Super Power Baby Shower*, and director of the award-winning erotic documentary series *Doing it Online*. Currently, she serves as Co-Executive Director for Gender Justice League.

KATHLEEN P. LAMOTHE is a white, able-bodied, kinky, femme, transsexual performance artist living with the simultaneous gift and curse of an ADHD brain. She currently resides on unceded Coast Salish territory (Vancouver), after having been raised in occupied Mohawk (Montreal) and Algonquin (Ottawa) territories. When she's not pissing off the gaygeousie or aiming her hyperfocus superpowers towards dense journal articles about cognitive neuroscience, she can be found going to 12-step meetings, getting tattooed, practicing mindfulness and compassion meditation, and ultimately challenging people's notions about what a "good" or "respectable" trans woman is.

G.B. LINDSEY's first love has always been writing: as a child, she cultivated such diverse goals as becoming "a cowgirl and a writer" or "a paleontologist and a writer." Aside from her salacious affair with the horror genre, she loves to write sci-fi, romance, historical fiction, and short stories. Her day job is in kidney transplant, but other interests include singing, reading voraciously, and period drama movie nights. She lives in California with her absolutely phenomenal cat.

MX. NILLIN LORE is an accomplished speaker who has provided LGBTQIA+ diversity training around the province of Saskatchewan, an established queer sexual pleasure and wellness advocate whose work has been featured worldwide, and a multiple award-winning blogger, placing eighth in Molly's Daily Kiss' Top 100 Sex Blogs of 2019 and sixth in Kinkly's Top 10 LGBTQ Blogs of 2019. Their short trans erotica story "Here Comes the Sun" was featured in 2019's *Best Lesbian Erotica of the Year Volume 4*. Look for them next as a co-author for the sexuality chapter in the Second Edition printing of *Trans Bodies, Trans Selves* from Oxford University Press.

AMANDA N currently resides in Pennsylvania; she hopes to one day escape. Having previously identified as bisexual, she married a man and had children. Upon leaving her marriage she realized she actually liked women and kink. With encouragement from a few friends, she wrote and submitted her first erotic story.

MICHELLE OSGOOD lives and writes in Vancouver, BC. She is best known for her series *The Better to Kiss You With*, including *The Better to Kiss You With*, *Huntsmen*, and *Moon Illusion*.

GISELLE RENARDE is an award-winning queer Canadian writer. Nominated Toronto's Best Author in *NOW Magazine*'s 2015 Readers' Choice Awards, her fiction has appeared in nearly 200 short story anthologies. Giselle's juicy novels include *Anonymous*, *Nanny State*, *Tragic Coolness*, *Cherry*, *In Shadow*, *Seven Kisses*, and *The Other Side of Ruth*.

JUNE AMELIA ROSE is an anarchist leatherdyke fiction writer and submissive transsexual femme living in Brooklyn. Her stories "Bootlicker" and "Porngirl, The Illustrious" were self-released as zines to cult praise. Her writing has also been featured in *FIST: A Zine for Leatherdykes*. She has edited four books so far, ranging from memoirs about underground punk music to novels about lesbian teenage sexuality. She is currently at work on her first novel, as well as a collection of essays. Follow her on Twitter and Instagram (@anarcho_slut) for more writing and depravity.

ABOUT THE EDITOR

SINCLAIR SEXSMITH (they/them) is "the best-known butch erotica writer whose kinky, groundbreaking stories have turned on countless queer women," who "is in all the books, wins all the awards, speaks at all the panels and readings, knows all the stuff, and writes for all the places" (Autostraddle).

They have written at sugarbutch.net since 2006, recognized by numerous places as one of the Top Sex Blogs. Sinclair's gender theory and queer erotica is widely published online and in more than thirty anthologies, including *Best Lesbian Erotica 2006, 2007, 2009, 2011, 2014, and 2016, Sometimes She Lets Me: Best Butch/Femme Erotica, Take Me There: Trans and Genderqueer Erotica, The Harder She Comes: Butch/Femme Erotica, The Big Book of Orgasms: 69 Sexy Stories, The Sexy Librarian's Dirty 30, Me & My Boi: Queer Erotic Stories, Paradigms of Power: Styles of Master/slave Relationships, Queer: A Reader for Writers, The Remedy: Trans and Queer Healthcare, Queering Sexual Violence: Radical Voices from Within the Anti-Violence Movement, Persistence: All Ways Butch and*

Femme, Nonbinary: Memoirs of Gender and Identity, and others.

Sinclair has edited *Best Lesbian Erotica of the Year Volume 4, Erotix: Literary Journal of Somatics, Best Lesbian Erotica 2012,* and *Say Please: Lesbian BDSM Erotica.* In 2015, they published a six novella series, which included *Bois Will Be Bois: Butch/Butch Erotica* and *The Dyke In Psych Class: Butch/Femme Erotica.* Their short story collection, *Sweet & Rough: Queer Kink Erotica,* was a 2015 finalist for the Lambda Literary Award, and they were awarded the National Leather Association Cynthia Slater Nonfiction Article Award in 2015 and the National Leather Association John Preston Short Story Award 2016 and 2019.

They have taught kink, gender, sexuality, relationship, and writing workshops online and throughout the US and Canada. Sinclair is also a facilitator and co-founder of Body Trust, a somatic arts collective. All of their work centers around studies of power and the body—individual, interpersonal, and institutional. They identify as a white non-binary butch dominant, a survivor, and an introvert, and they live on unceded Ohlone land in Oakland, California, with their boy. Follow all their writings at patreon.com/mrsexsmith.